THE TIME
OF THE PEACOCK

—

MENA ABDULLAH

& RAY MATHEW

INTRODUCTION BY THOMAS SHAPCOTT

ETT IMPRINT

Exile Bay

This edition published by ETT Imprint, Exile Bay in 2025

First published in Australia by Angus & Robertson Publishers in 1965
Reprinted 1969, 1970, 1973, 1974, 1977, 1990, 1992

First published by ETT imprint in 2019

First electronic edition ETT Imprint 2019

These stories were first published in *The Bulletin*, with the exception of
"The Babu from Bengal" and "A Long Way", which first appeared in
Quadrant and *Hemisphere* respectively

ISBN 978-1-923205-92-5 (pbk)
ISBN 978-1-925706-89-5 (ebk)

Cover design by Tom Thompson

INTRODUCTION

These stories first flashed and danced in the brittle newsprint of The Bulletin in the late 1950s. Those were the years when that dying weekly (which was to be sold to Consolidated Press in 1960) had a last creative fling in poetry and prose. The rare world of Mena Abdullah's Indian childhood in the Namoi-Gwydir area of New South Wales caught something new. We who subscribed to The Bulletin waited for the next story to appear. And the next.

In those years 'multiculturalism' had not been invented. This does not mean to say that the impact of postwar migration was not being felt, or expressed, or that prewar migration patterns were not already part of our secret heritage. Some literature, like Xavier Herbert's 1939 novel Capricornia had already raised challenges to ideas of a 'white' society. Other writing, particularly poetry and the short story, works (and worked) differently. At the time Mena Abdullah's poems and stories began to appear in the pages of The Bulletin, Eric Schlunke's Riverina studies of German families were well known and Enid Gollscheswky, writing of settlement farmers, had also been published and anthologised. It is true, though, that in the 1950s the official concept of 'assimilation' still haunted ways of approaching what we now can affirm as a genuine multiplicity of cultural responses to the environment.

Mena Kashmiri Abdullah first attracted attention with a poem, 'The Red Koran' published in The Bulletin on 15 June 1954.This was picked up and given prominence in the Angus & Robertson annual anthology, *Aust-*

ralian Poetry edited in 1955 by James McAuley. It was the first poem in the volume and its ballad-like observation was matched by the undoubted novelty of the subject matter:

He came to our farm when I was small,
From our perch in the top of the fig-tree tall
We watched him, a small dot on the hill,
Till he rounded the bend by the timber-mill.
He had the build of the frontier race,
But there was peace in his gentle face
And he called out the Muslim greeting prayer,
When he saw the four of us waiting there—
The wandering hadji, Muhummed Khan,
And clutched to his breast was the red Koran.

Even to approach such a simple poem from this end of the twentieth century is to be reminded how far the shadow of the bush ballad tradition still stretched, mid-century. It is also to be reminded that there were already generations of people living in this country whose ancestry (and cultural identity) went back as far as that of most of their Anglo-Celtic neighbours. Mena Abdullah writes of an Indian family (Kashmiri Brahmin mother, Bengali Muslim father) which is well established, if isolated. If there is a nostalgia for lost culture there is also a relaxed acceptance of the here and now: 'our perch in the top of the fig-tree' and 'the bend by the timber-mill'.

Only three of the stories appeared in *The Bulletin* under Mena Abdullah's sole name (Grandfather Tiger, 12 December 1956, The Dragon of Kashmir, 4 March 1959 and High Maharajah, 24 June 1959). All the others were published as co-authored with Ray Mathew.

In the early 1950s Ray Mathew was a young poet of lyric verve and the leading exponent, after Douglas Stewart, of the now discounted genre of verse-drama. He was the Michael Gow of his time. By 1960 he was to become, as a short story writer, something of the Frank Moorhouse of his generation. His book of stories *A Bohemian Affair* (1961), with its emphasis on Sydney cafe life, certainly anticipates the same hedonistic and intellectual games-playing.

Mathew worked for the CSIRO from 1952 to 1954 and it is undoubtedly through this connection that he met Mena Abdullah, also employed there.

His influence on her style and approach to subject matter is most clearly felt in the development of lyrical poise in her work, and in an honesty towards the expression of vulnerability as a tool in breaking down barriers of unfamiliarity or difference. In the short stories of *The Time of the Peacock* these techniques have been refined to a telling degree.

Although Mena Abdullah published some thirteen poems in *The Bulletin* between 1954 and 1959, only two were anthologised in the landmark Angus & Robertson annual surveys. The second of these, called 'The Prison', appeared in *Australian Poetry 1957*, edited that year by Nancy Keesing. It is perhaps worth quoting fully, to illustrate the technical advance in her writing skills under the impact of Ray Mathew's then potent lyricism:

I built a house of silence,
My stormy heart to hide,
And day and night a peacock guard
Was ever at my side.

I whispered to the peacock,
'All vows men make are lies,'
The peacock only looked at me
With burning anguished eye

In that grey house of silence
No blessings came to me:
No songs, no words of comfort;
Time stretched an empty sea.

And when there came temptation
From those cold walls to run
The shadow of the peacock
Was between me and the sun.

One day as I was leaning
From the window of my room,
I saw, around the crescent creek,
The warm spring flowers in bloom.

I said 'The sun's gold tear-drops
Shine on the wattle tree.'
The peacock turned his head away
And would not look at me.

Then I, in utter loneliness,
Sank weeping to the floor;
My peacock, Pride, was vanquished
And you came within my door.

In his third collection, *South of the Equator* (1961), Mathew included a poem called 'Star Cast'. It seems a direct response and counterpoint to that Mena Abdullah poem. It is also a poem about cross-cultural difficulties, especially in an era when the White Australia Policy was in force:

She calls them half-caste children, I call them love.
To me they are the thing not her not me,
The spring that is the river is the sea.

The peacock-pride that struts behind her talk
Is alien bird to me; I can't belong
Where birds are patterns in a formal song.

My birds are strong shapes, funny, odd; themselves
To take their chance in trees, to live and die,
Open to all the weathers of the sky.

In the simplest sense, then, the stories in *The Time of the Peacock* do arise from a creative interaction between Mena Abdullah and Ray Mathew. But their essence—their more than essence—is triumphantly hers. 'Star Cast' might be a poem that simplifies attitudes and problems, but it also emphasises the world-view of Mena Abdullah that we are so haunted by in the stories. I think Mathew would never claim to be more than a facilitator in their realisation. It was well known at the time that joint authorship made it easier for payment of royalties to go to Ray, who was then struggling as a freelance writer. Mena remained with the CSIRO.

When these stories first appeared in scattered issues of *The Bulletin* in the 1950s I read them and was moved by their poignant celebration of an environment I knew well, the New England landscape. I was even more haunted by their subtle delineation of an unfamiliar family made magical through the holiness of small details. What held me was the essential fragility of childhood, but that childhood emphasised a hundred-fold because it was under threat by much greater forces than processes of change and growth.

The magic of this world is in the family, and the family binds into itself both safety and the greater vulnerability. Strangely, it is not until Rodney Hall's 1988 novella *Captivity Captive* that a similar tightly-knit family isolation so integrates a book. But there it is a gothic tale of horror, whereas in Mena Abdullah's world a more fragile and celebratory intention is sustained.

Re-reading these stories after more than thirty years I was taken by surprise again, as much by my own reaction as by the craft of the writing. I was as vulnerable to their intentions upon me as I had been as a young man. This tells something of their technical accomplishment as much as it does of the subject matter and the dangerous balancing acts with themes of innocence, infant fevers and the pathos of first days at school. The stories could be as sentimental as the worst of Lawson, universal themes— new, still, after more than a generation.

In the intervening thirty-five or so years, much has changed in Australian society and culture.

What we first read as essentially elegant evocations of the exotic world within our own world, we now see as landmark explorations of ethnic difference and identity. *The Time of the Peacock* must stand with Judah Waten's 1952 *Alien Son* as one of the turning points in our cultural development.

Mena Abdullah (and Ray Mathew) were being honest to their delineation, and perhaps discovery, of authentic experience. The world of that Muslim-Hindu child speaks of exile and the self, of the confines of family and its great sustaining strengths. It offers subtle lessons in alternative social environments. It also teaches us that the best writing can be powerfully moving while at the same time confronting us with issues that, over time, increase in relevance. *The Time of the Peacock* is a book that has more to say to more people now than it had when, in the 1950s, the stories first appeared.

Thomas Shapcott

CONTENTS

THE TIME
OF THE PEACOCK

WHEN I was little everything was wonderful; the world was our farm and we were all loved. Rashida and Lal and I, Father and our mother, Ama: we loved one another and everything turned to good.

I remember in autumn, how we burned the great baskets of leaves by the Gwydir and watched the fires burning in the river while Ama told us stories of Krishna the Flute-player and his moving mountains. And when the fires had gone down and the stories were alive in our heads we threw cobs of corn into the fires and cooked them. One for each of us— Rashida and Lal and I, Father and our mother.

Winter I remember, when the frost bit and stung and the wind pulled our hair. At night by the fire in the warmth of the house, we could hear the dingoes howling.

Then it was spring and the good year was born again. The sticks of the jasmine vine covered themselves with flowers.

One spring I remember was the time of the peacock when I learnt the word secret and began to grow up. After that spring everything somehow was different, was older. I was not little any more, and the baby came.

I had just learnt to count. I thought I could count anything. I counted fingers and toes, the steps and the windows, even the hills. But this day in spring the hills were wrong.

There should have been five. I knew that there should have been five. I counted them over and over—"*Ek, do, tin, punch*"—but it was no good. There was one too many, a strange hill, a left-over. It looked familiar, and I knew it, but it made more than five and worried me. I thought of Krishna and the mountains that moved to protect the cowherds, the travellers lost because of them, and I was frightened because it seemed to me that our hills had moved.

I ran through the house and out into the garden to tell Ama the thing that Krishna had done and to ask her how we could please him. But when I saw her I forgot all about them; I was as young as that. I just stopped and jumped, up and down.

She was standing there, in her own garden, the one with the Indian flowers, her own little walled-in country. Her hands were joined together in front of her face, and her lips were moving. On the ground, in front of the Kashmiri rosebush; in front of the tuberoses, in front of the pomegranate-tree, she had placed little bowls of shining milk. I jumped to see them. Now I knew why I was running all the time and skipping, why I wanted to sing out and to count everything in the world.

"It is spring," I shouted to Ama. "Not nearly-spring! Not almost-spring! But really-spring! Will the baby come soon?"

I asked her. "Soon?"

"Soon, Impatience, soon."

I laughed at her and jumped up and clapped my hands together over the top of my head.

"I am as big as that," I said. "I can do anything." And I hopped on one leg to the end of the garden where the peacock lived. "Shah-Jehan!" I said to him — that was his name. "It is spring and the baby is coming, pretty Shah-Jehan." But he didn't seem interested. "Silly old Shah-Jehan," I said. "Don't you know anything? I can count ten."

He went on staring with his goldy eye at me. He *was* a silly bird. Why, he had to stay in the garden all day, away from the rooster. He couldn't run everywhere the way that I could. He couldn't do anything.

"Open your tail," I told him. "Go on, open your tail." And we went on staring at one another till I felt sad.

"Rashida is right," I said to him. "You will never open your tail like the bird on the fan. But why don't you try? Please, pretty Shah-Jehan." But he just went on staring as though he would never open his tail, and while I looked at him sadly I remembered how he had come to us.

He could lord it now and strut in the safety of the garden, but I remembered how the Lascar brought him to the farm, in a bag, like a cabbage, with his feathers drooping and his white tail dirty.

The Lascar came to the farm, a seaman on the land, a dark face in a white country. How he smiled when he saw us— Rashida and me swinging on the gate. How he chattered to Ama and made her laugh and cry. How he had shouted about the curries that she gave him.

And when it was time to go, with two basins of curry tied up in cloth and packed in his bag, he gave the bird to Ama, gave it to her while she said nothing, not even "thank you". She only looked at him.

"What is it?" we said as soon as he was far enough away. "What sort of bird?"

"It is a peacock," said Ama, very softly. "He has come to us from India."

"It is not like the peacock on your Kashmiri fan," I said. "It is only a sort of white."

"The peacock on the fan is green and blue and gold and has a tail like a fan," said Rashida. "This is not a peacock at all. Anyone can see that."

"Rashida," said Ama, "Rashida! The eldest must not be too clever. He is a white peacock. He is too young to open his tail. He is a peacock from India."

"Ama," I said, "Make him, make him open his tail."

"I do not think," she said, "I do not think he will ever open his tail in this country."

"No," said Father that night, "he will never open his tail in Australia."

"No," said Uncle Seyed next morning, "he will never open his tail without a hen-bird near."

But we had watched him—Rashida and Lal and I—had watched him for days and days until we had grown tired of watching and he had grown sleek and shiny and had found his place in the garden.

"Won't you ever open your tail?" I asked him again. "Not now that it's spring?" But he wouldn't even try, not even try to look interested, so I went away from him and looked for someone to talk to.

The nurse-lady who was there to help Ama and who was pink like an apple and almost as round was working in the kitchen.

"The baby is coming soon," I told her. "Now that it's spring."

"Go on with you." she laughed. "Go on."

So I did, until I found Rashida sitting in a window-sill with a book in front of her. It was the nurse-lady's baby-book. "What are you doing?"

"I am reading," she said. "This is the baby-book. I am reading how to look after the baby."

"You can't read," I said. "You know you can't read." Rashida refused to answer. She just went on staring at the book, turning pages.

"But you can't read!" I shouted at her. "You can't."

She finished running her eye down the page. "I am not reading words," she said. "I know what the book tells. I am reading things."

"But you know, you know you can't read." I stamped away from her, cranky as anything, out of the house, past the window where Rashida was sitting—so cleverly—down to the vegetable patch where I could see Lal. He was digging with a trowel.

What are you doing?" I said, not very pleasantly.

"I am digging," said Lal. "I am making a garden for my new baby brother."

How did you know? How did you all know? I was going to tell you." I was almost crying. "Anyway," I said, "it might not be a brother."

"Oh yes, it will," said Lal. "We have girls."

"I'll dig, too," I said, laughing, and suddenly happy again. "I'll help you. We'll make a big one."

"Digging is man's work," said Lal. "I'm a man. You're a girl."

"You're a baby," I said. "You're only four." And I threw some dirt at him, and went away.

Father was making a basket of sticks from the plum-tree. He used to put crossed sticks on the ground, squat in the middle of them, and weave other sticks in and out of them until a basket had grown up round him. All I could see were his shoulders and the back of his turban as I crept up behind him, to surprise him.

But he was not surprised. "I knew it would be you," he said. I scowled at him then, but he only laughed the way that he always did.

"Father—" I began in a questioning voice that made him groan. Already I was called the Australian one, the questioner. "Father," I said, "why do peacocks have beautiful tails?"

He tugged at his beard. "Their feet are ugly," he said. "Allah has given them tails so that no one will look at their feet."

"But Shah-Jehan," I said, and Father bent his head down over his weaving. "Everyone looks at his feet. His tail never opens."

"Yes," said Father definitely, as though that explained everything, and I began to cry: it was that sort of day, laughter and tears. I suppose it was the first day of spring.

"What is it, what is it?" said Father.

"Everything," I told him. "Shah-Jehan won't open his tail, Rashida pretends she can read, Lal won't let me dig. I'm nothing. And it's spring. Ama is putting out the milk for the snakes, and I counted—" But Father was looking so serious that I never told him what I had counted.

"Listen," he said. "You are big now, Nimmi. I will tell you a secret."

"What is secret?"

He sighed. "It is what is ours," he said. "Something we know but do not tell, or share with one person only in the world."

"With me!" I begged. "With me!"

"Yes," he said, "with you. But no crying or being nothing. This is to make you a grown-up person."

"Please," I said to him, "please." And I loved him then so much that I wanted to break the cage of twigs and hold him.

"We are Muslims," he said. "But your mother has a mark on her forehead that shows that once she was not. She was a Brahmin and she believed all the stories of Krishna and Siva."

"I know that," I said, "and the hills—"

"Monkey, quiet," he commanded. "But now Ama is a Muslim, too. Only, she remembers her old ways. And she puts out the milk in the spring."

"For the snakes," I said. "So they will love us. and leave us from harm."

"But there are no snakes in the garden," said Father.

"But they drink the milk," I told him. "Ama says—"

"If the milk were left, the snakes would come," said Father. "And they must not come, because there is no honour in snakes. They would strike you or Rashida or little Lal or even Ama. So—and this is the secret that no one must know but you and me—I go to the garden in the night and empty the dishes of milk. And this way I have no worry and you have no harm and Ama's faith is not hurt. But you must never tell."

"Never, never tell," I assured him.

All that day I was kind to Lal, who was only a baby and not grown up, and I held my head up high in front of Rashida, who was clever but had no secret. All of that day I walked in a glory full of my secret. I even felt cleverer than Ama, who knew everything but must never, never know this.

She was working that afternoon on her quilt. I looked at the crochet pictures in the little squares of it.

"Here is a poinsettia," I said.

"Yes," said Ama. "And here is—"

"It's Shah-Jehan! With his tail open."

"Yes," said Ama, "so it is, and here is a rose for the baby."

"When will the baby come?" I asked her. "Not soon, but when?"

"Tonight, tomorrow night," said Ama, "the next."

"Do babies always come at night?"

"Mine, always," said Ama. "There is the dark and the waiting, and then the sun on our faces. And the scent of jasmine, even here." And she looked at her garden.

"But, Ama—"

"No questions, Nimmi. My head is buzzing. No questions today."

That night I heard a strange noise, a harsh cry. "Shah- Jehan!" I said. I jumped out of bed and ran to the window. I stood on a chair and looked out to the garden.

It was moonlight, the moon so big and low that I thought I could lean out and touch it, and there—looking sad, and white as frost in the moonlight—stood Shah-Jehan.

"Shah-Jehan, little brother," I said to him, "you must not feel about your feet. Think of your tail, pretty one, your beautiful tail."

And then, as I was speaking, he lifted his head and slowly, slowly opened his tail—like a fan, like a fan of lace that was as white as the moon. O Shah-Jehan! It was as if you had come from the moon.

My throat hurt, choked, so that my breath caught and I shut my eyes. When I opened them it was all gone: the moon was the moon and Shah-Je-han was a milky-white bird with his tail drooping and his head bent.

In the morning the nurse-lady woke us. "Get up," she said. "Guess what? In the night, a sister! The dearest, sweetest, baby sister…Now, up with you."

"No brother," said Lal. "No baby brother."

We laughed at him, Rashida and I, and ran to see the baby. Ama was lying, very still and small, in the big bed. Her long plait of black hair stretched out across the white pillow. The baby was in the old cradle and we peered down at her. Her tiny fists groped on the air towards us. But Lal would not look at her. He climbed onto the bed and crawled over to Ama.

"No boy," he said sadly. "No boy to play with."

Ama stroked his hair. "My son," she said. "I am sorry, little son."

"Can we change her?" he said. "For a boy?"

"She is a gift from Allah," said Ama. "You can never change gifts."

Father came in from the dairy, his face a huge grin, he made a chuckling noise over the cradle and then sat on the bed.

"Missus," he said in the queer English that always made the nurse-lady laugh, "this one little fellow, eh?"

"Big," said Ama. "Nine pounds." And the nurse-lady nodded proudly.

"What wrong with this fellow?" said Father, scooping Lal up in his arm. "What wrong with you, eh?"

"No boy," said Lal. "No boy to talk to."

"Ai! Ai!" lamented Father, trying to change his expression. "Too many girls here," he said. "Better we drown one. Which one we drown, Lal? Which one, eh?"

Rashida and I hurled ourselves at him, squealing with delight. "Not me! Not me!" we shouted while the nurse-lady tried to hush us.

"You are worse than the children," she said to Father. "Far worse." But then she laughed, and we all did—even the baby made a noise.

But what was the baby to be called? We all talked about it. Even Uncle Seyed came in and leant on the doorpost while names were talked over and over.

At last Father lifted the baby up and looked into her big dark eyes. "What was the name of your sister?" he asked Uncle Seyed. "The little one, who followed us everywhere? The little one with the beautiful eyes?"

"Jamila," said Uncle Seyed. "She was Jamila."

So that was to be her first name, Jamila, after the little girl who was alive in India when Father was a boy and he and Uncle Seyed had decided to become friends like brothers. And her second name was Shahnaz, which means the Heart's Beloved.

And then I remembered. "Shah-Jehan," I said. "He can open his tail. I saw him last night, when everyone was asleep."

"You couldn't see in the night," said Rashida. "You dreamt it, baby."

"No, I didn't. It was bright moon."

"You dreamt it, Nimmi," said Father. "A peacock wouldn't open his tail in this country."

"I didn't dream it," I said in a little voice that didn't sound very certain: Father was always right. "I'll count Jamila's fingers," I said before Rashida could say anything else about the peacock. "*Ek, do, tin, panch,*" I began.

"You've left out *cha,*" said Father.

"Oh yes, I forgot. I forgot it. *Ek, do, tin, cha, panch*— she has five," I said.

"Everyone has five," said Rashida.

"Show me," said Lal. And while Father and Ama were showing him the baby's fingers and toes and telling him how to count them, I crept out on the veranda where I could see the hills.

I counted them quickly. "*Ek, do, tin, cha, panch.*" There were only five, not one left over. I was so excited that I felt the closing in my throat again. "I didn't dream it," I said. "I couldn't dream the pain. I did see it, I did. I have another secret now. And only five hills. *Ek, do, tin, cha, panch.*"

They never changed again. I was grown up.

BECAUSE
OF THE RUSILLA

THE whole day—the trip to town, the nigger word, the singing kettle—was because of the Rusilla. It had flown away.

It was a small bird and of no use to the farm, but it was Lal's and its loss was a tragic thing.

It was Rashida who found it, though, Rashida and I. It was in the grass by the creek, shining red and green and fluttering to get out of the long creek grass. I saw it first and I pointed to it. But Rashida stalked it and caught it. Then we carried it back to Father. That's to say, Rashida carried it. I wanted to and I had the right because I saw it first, but Rashida didn't offer it and I couldn't ask her. She was older than I was and she had the right to decide. And besides, even though we were children on the banks of the Gwydir, we were still Punjabis and Punjabis do not beg. Even a little child like Lal knew that. And so did I. Rashida carried it. Father looked at the bird. "Young and weak," he said. "Young and weak. It will mostly die."

"Yes," said Rashida in a proud voice, holding herself up to look at life as a Punjabi should. "It will die."

She gave the bird to me then and I took it gladly. I held it tightly, too tightly probably. Its wings flapped at my hands and I could feel, under the wings and the feathers, a wild beating like the noise you hear at night when your ear is on the pillow, and I knew it was the bird's heart beating.

So I held it more gently than before, in a cage of fingers. "What bird?" I said. "What sort of bird? What name?" Father looked at me and frowned. I was always asking names, more names than there were words for. I was the dreamy one, the one he called the Australian.

"Rusilla," he said at last. "It is a bird called Rusilla."

"Rusilla?" I said. "Rusilla." It was a good name and I was satisfied.

I took it home and showed it to Lal, who was only four. "I have a Rusilla," I said. "It is a very strange bird, young and weak, and it will mostly die, but you can help me feed it. Get grass-seeds and blackberries. Grass-seeds like these."

He pottered away gravely while I put the bird in a chicken-coop that had been left by some accident in the garden. And from that day Lal and I hunted the garden, gathering and sorting, to feed the Rusilla.

The garden was a strange place and lovely. It was our mother's place, Ama's own place. Outside its lattice walls was the farmyard with its fowls and goats (Sulieman the rooster and Yasmin the nanny), and beyond that was Father's place, the wool-sheds and the yards, and beyond that the hills with their changing faces and their Australianness. We had never been to them, and Ama — that was our word for "mother"; *ama* means love—Ama told us they were very strange. But everything was strange to Ama, except the garden.

Inside its lattice walls grew the country that she knew. There were tuberose and jasmine, white violets and the pink Kashmiri roses whose buds grew clenched, like baby hands. The garden was cool and sweet and full of rich scent. Even the kitchen smell of curry and of ghee was lost and had no meaning in that place. There was Shah-Jehan the white peacock, too. And other birds came there, free birds of their own will, the magpie day and night to wake us at morning and to bed us at night, and a shining black bird that Indians call "kokila" and Australians call "koel". But these were singing birds that came and went, came and went. For the Rusilla, the garden was a cage.

It was a cage for Lal, too. He was gentle and small and the only son because another, an elder one, had merely opened his eyes to die. Ama and Father were afraid for Lal; they kept him in the garden. Rashida and I could run mad by the creek, bare feet and screaming voices, but Lal could not go out without a grown-up. He had to live in the garden with the baby, Jamila, who was only six months and who spent all her day sucking her fist and watching the rose-leaves move on the sky or in sleeping and sleeping. She was not much good for a boy to play with, even a delicate boy of four. To Lal the Rusilla was a bird, a friend, from heaven.

And it was entirely his. As soon as it was well I lost interest in it and grew sick of the garden. I told him he could have it, that it was no use anyway, and that it would never do anything but walk round in its cage and make whistling noises. Lal didn't care. He loved it and watched it for hours.

And then one morning, just like any other morning, we woke up and it was gone. The door of the cage was open and Salome the cat had disappeared. The magpies went on singing as on any other morning and Lal shook his fist at them as he'd seen Father shake his fist at the sun. And he cried.

How he cried! Tears down his face, and no sound. And all the time he ran round the garden—now quick, now slow— looking, looking. He didn't even speak.

"Ama," said Rashida, "let Lal come to the swamp with us."

"We'll show him the ducks," I said. "Baby ones, Lal. Learning to swim."

But it was no good. Ama told Father it was no good, and Father, smiling a little, nursed Lal for a long time. But the tears were still there and all afternoon Father went round the paddocks with a net trying to find a Rusilla. But the bird from heaven had gone and it seemed that there was no other like it in the world. It was just as Lal had said.

We children slept in the same room and that night Rashida and I lay for a long time listening to Lal, waiting for him to cry himself to sleep. But it was no good. We climbed out of the big bed and went over to him.

"Lal-baba," said Rashida. "Don't cry. Don't cry," she said again, and I saw that there were tears on her cheek and I began to sniffle and to feel my eyes filling.

"Don't cry, don't cry, don't cry," I said. And then I was crying, very loudly, and Rashida, with tears on her face, was disgusted with me, and Ama, as she always was when we needed her, was suddenly there with a lamp. She picked up Lal and held him like a very little baby.

"What noise!" she said. "Go to bed." And when she had seen us safely in, she sat on a chair with Lal and talked to him in her soft Indian voice, so soft that the words were hardly words they seemed so true. And yet we heard them. "My son," she said. "My son, no tears. Allah makes birds to fly. No tears. It is cruel, it is cruel to stay in a cage when you have the wings and the heart to fly. No tears. You cannot hold a bird. You cannot hold things, anything, my son."

Lal leant against her. I could tell that his face was hot from crying by the way Ama rubbed her cheek on him. Her face was creased and tired, but suddenly she smiled and looked beautiful.

"Tomorrow," she said, "Seyed can take you in the wagon and you can see the town."

"Me, too, Ama? Me, too?" Rashida and I jumped up in bed. None of us had ever been to town. Lal stopped crying.

"Yes, sleepers," said Ama. "All of you." And she took Lal in her arms into her own room while Rashida and I whispered excitedly about Uncle Seyed, the Rusilla, and the town.

Uncle Seyed came the next day with the wagon. It was always used on town days, but it was very old. It belonged to the time when father first came to Australia. He had nothing but the clothes he wore and the Koran tied in a red handkerchief which he used for a prayer mat. With the money from his first jobs he bought the wagon. Faded, but still proud, the letters on the side said: MUHUMMAD DIN — LICENSED HAWKER.

We'd been in it lots of times, but never to go to town, never to go to town. We hopped about in the back like birds while Seyed worried about us falling out and eventually tried talking to us in an effort to keep us still.

"Good land that," he said. He always spoke to us in English, his sort of English. "Long time ago I want your father to buy it, but no. He want go back home, get marry. I tell him he too young get marry, but no." Seyed shook his head and Rashida laughed. She knew that father was forty when he married. Seyed shook his head again. "Always your father wanting to get marry."

"When will you get married, Uncle Seyed?" asked Rashida.

"Plenty time yet," said Seyed, who was in his fifties. "Plenty time yet" "I will marry you," I said. And then I thought a bit "Soon," I added, and Rashida laughed.

And so the talking, the good time, went while the sun got big and the paddocks got small and the houses came closer to one another. By the time we drove into the town we had no words to say.

Seyed stopped the wagon in the grass at the side of the road and lifted us down.

"Better you wait in shade," he said. "No run on road. Back in few minutes." He shook a warning finger and left us.

It was only a small town and we looked at it, looked hard.

"What's that?" I said pointing to a high, high, brick building.

"Only a Jesus-house," said Rashida knowledgeably, but she looked at it as curiously as Lal and I.

"Look!" said Lal suddenly. "Rusilla."

We looked. It was a stone rooster near a stone man on the side of the building. It seemed very wonderful to us and we stood staring at it while Lal crowed quietly about Rusilla, the bird from heaven, and how it lived on a house.

It was because of the Rusilla and the stone man that we saw no one approaching. Suddenly they were there, white children—a big boy, a middle-sized girl, and a little boy. We stared at them. They stared at us.

"What y' wearin' y' pyjamas in the street f'r?" said the big boy.

"What y' wearin' y' pyjamas in the street f'r?" said the girl.

We stared at them and I kept saying the question over in my head like a song. I didn't know what it meant except that it meant our clothes. We were all dressed alike in the sulwa-kameez, a sort of loose tunic and baggy cotton trousers caught in at the ankles, serviceable, cheap to buy and easy to make. It was easy to wash, too. And Ama had washed them as white as anything. Why were they pointing, and singing, and saying such sharp pointy words?

"Nigger," sang the big boy. "Nigger, nigger, pull the trigger."

"Nigger, nigger, pull the trigger," said the others. They were all saying it, singing it, like a game.

"Game!" cried Lal. He ran forward. He lived in a world of women, an only son, and here were boys. He ran to meet them.

The big boy caught him around the waist and gave him a throw that sent him backwards to the ground. I saw him there and looked at him sitting up surprised and felt my legs shaking and my eyes sore.

"*Sur ka bucha!*" said Rashida. "*Sur ka bucha!*" she screamed and flung herself at the boy, her clenched fists banging at him. I was horrified because that means "son of a pig", and it was a terrible phrase to us, but I followed her, crying, '*Sur! Sur!*" And, jumping at the girl, I grabbed two handfuls of hair.

We were all there fighting—thumping and kicking and scratching, with Lal sitting amazed on the ground—when Seyed came back.

"Ai! Ai!" he cried as he turned the comer and broke into a run. At the sound of his voice and the sight of his turban, the fighting stopped and the strangers ran away. Rashida stood looking after them, still shaking with anger and strength, but I looked towards Seyed wanting him to come to us.

He asked us what had happened and I held up a fist that had some blonde hair in it and started to cry. And, of course, that set Lal off; he couldn't let any of us cry alone. Seyed was distraught, but tried hard to be calm. He picked Lal up and dusted him. He retied the ribbon in my hair, a clumsy bow, but I loved him for it. And he told Rashida, who was being too proud to cry, to wipe her nose.

"Wipe good," he said.

"Take us home," commanded Rashida. "Take us home now."

"Business at bank. No go home yet." Even as he said it he must have seen that Rashida would begin to cry, too, so he hurried us back into the wagon and drove us down the street. We none of us looked out. We crouched in the back.

"Where are we going?" I said, but in a very little voice that Seyed couldn't hear. Rashida sat up and looked.

"We are not going home," she said and her voice trembled. But she stayed sitting up, looking proud, and as I lay there crying into Lal's hair I thought that she looked very like father and wondered if anyone would ever think that about me.

Seyed took us to a cottage on the other side of town where a white lady lived. He told us to stay with her and to give her no trouble because she was a friend, and that if we were good he would come back and take us home soon. Then he went away, into the town, while we stood stock-still in the garden and looked at the ground.

"I don't know your names," said the lady. Rashida was the eldest. "I am Rashida Bani. This is my sister, Nimmi Kushil. And this is my brother—the only son— Lal Muhummad. We come from Simla Farm."

"I know it," said the lady. "I knew it, and I knew your father before you were thought of." We stared at her with respect; she must be very old. We could not imagine a time when father and Ama had not thought of us, and longed for us.

She took us into the house and like a very wise woman indeed went on with her work and left us alone. We walked round slowly, in sight of one another, and looked at everything. Then we decided.

Rashida stood by the piano. She struck a key. A miracle happened. A note came loud and clear. Then it died away till no matter how carefully you listened it was gone. Only you knew that it would never go because you had it in your mind and in your heart. She struck another one and, after the note started, sang with it. There were two notes then, the same and different, but again the piano note faded away into your mind. Lal laughed and I stood listening and Rashida, sure of herself, sat by the piano and began picking at the keys. High notes some of them were and some were low, and she sang with all of those she could. She was always singing at home and she knew all of Ama's songs.

I sat on the floor near her and turned over the pages of a magazine I'd taken from a big pile of papers. The pages shone and the ink smelt beautifully. There were big pictures, and I put my head close to them to see them and smell them and know them properly.

Lal began talking to a black cat that was sleeping under the table. He talked happily for a long time, but the cat woke up and arched his back and stretched himself and walked off into another room. Lal went after him.

Suddenly there was a whistling noise and a shout from Lal. Such a shout! Rashida and I jumped up and ran after him. He was in the kitchen, standing in front of the stove. On it was a kettle, a kettle that sang. He pointed to it.

"Look," he said. "Listen." We were astounded. We stood wide-eyed as Lal. A kettle that sang, sang high and shrill!

"Like a locust," said Rashida. "Like a bird."

"Magic," said I.

"Rusilla," said Lal.

The lady came in and took the kettle off the stove. "It sings to say that it is boiling," she said. "I saw Seyed coming up the street and put it on to make some tea."

So we all sat down to tea and scones and chattered like relations. We loved the lady now, the kind lady with the piano and the papers, the cat and the kettle. We told her about the farm and the three kangaroos that Ama fed, about the Rusilla and the garden where Lal lived, about Jamila the baby and the long time she was asleep. We told her everything and she listened and laughed and smiled while Seyed drank cups of black tea full of sugar. And when Lal could get a word in, he talked, too. He talked to Seyed and told him, very gravely, about the wonderful kettle that sang like a bird.

Then we all went out to the wagon. We stood for a moment in the garden to say good-bye and the lady, picking a rose from each bush, gave a strong red one to Rashida and a dear pink one to me. "For good girls," she said. Then she looked at Lal and shook her head. "I can't give flowers to a man."

Lal's face fell and we were all afraid he would cry, but he just looked sad and Seyed lifted him into the wagon.

"Don't go," said the lady. "Wait." And she went inside.

We were all in the wagon ready to go when she came out. She was carrying the kettle.

"This is for you," she said and held it towards Lal. "I have two others for myself."

Lal took it, but Seyed was frowning at him and he half held it out for her to take back. Even Lal knew that Punjabi men do not accept gifts easily.

"Let him take it," said the lady. "A friend gives you what is already your own." Seyed thought about it and then smiled, a huge grin. "You Punjabi lady," he said.

So the kettle was Lal's. All the way home we held on to our presents, even when we fell asleep as we all did. But we woke up near home, not because of any sound or any difference, but only because of the nearness of home. We climbed up on to the seat near Seyed, who worried about us falling off and prayed loudly that we'd stay on until he got us to our father.

The sun was going down as we sighted home. It was the time that Father called the Glory of Allah. The day was burning itself out. The crows cawed and flapped their way towards the trees. There was a night noise of animals, drowsy and faint. There was a smell—growing stronger all the time—of wood-smoke and curry cooking. There was a white gleam down near the cowbail that was Father's turban and there, there in the doorway, with the baby on her arm and a lamp in her hand, was Ama.

"No more," said Seyed Muhummad solemnly and untruthfully as he helped us down from the wagon. "No more as long as Allah let me live will I take these devils in town."

We laughed at him, and we held our roses up for Ama to smell. But Lal pushed between us.

"Look, Ama," he said holding up his kettle. "Rusilla."

KUMARI

IT had been a strange week—the trip to town and all, the nigger word…
So strange a week that even I, young as I was, could see the whole of my
life as strange—a dark girl in a white man's country, a Punjabi Muslim in a
Christian land… So strange that I, who usually chattered and was known as
monkey, had fallen into silence.

And it was this week, when I needed her to listen when I felt like talking,
when I wanted her to bully and scold in her almost grown-up way, that
Rashida also became strange, different, not to be explained.

She was running from the kitchen where she should have been helping
and leaving Ama, our mother, and me to stalk the chillies and cut the
mangoes by ourselves.

"She is behaving like an Australian girl," said Ama.

"She is behaving lazy," I said.

But where was she going? Not to the garden to play, not to the creek to
paddle, not to the paddocks with Father.

"Where have you been?" I asked her.

No answer.

"Where have you been?"

"Secrets," said Rashida, and left me fuming.

But I *would* know. She was my sister and ought to share. She was not an
Australian girl and she ought to play with me. At night in our bedroom, I

told her, argued, demanded. I pleaded, begged, cried. "I don't want to know," I assured her. "You're only a little black pig, not grown up at all."

And even though I'd called her black, a word we were not allowed to use, even though I'd called her pig, which we thought the nastiest word a Muslim could say, she just smiled secrets and told me I was too little to be trusted.

And the next day I watched her. Ama was making the curry powder, and Rashida was supposed to be watching the coriander seeds and the cumin and the black peppers as they roasted. I was stalking the chillies, ready for salting.

Suddenly—almost I didn't see her and Ama's back was turned—Rashida was gone. I jumped up and ran after her. But she was very quick. She was not in the house, not in the garden. I went into the latticed yard that was Ama's Indian place, full of Kashmiri roses and pomegranates and jasmine and tuberose. Little brother Lal was there, digging at the garden in his messy way.

"Where's she gone?" I asked him. "Where's Rashida?"

Lal went on digging. "I don't watch girls." Already he had a Muslim man's contempt. "I'm working."

"You're only four!"

I was so angry that I reached up into the willow-tree where Shah-Jehan, our peacock, was sitting and made as if to pull his tail. He squawked. And Lal squawked, too, jumping to his feet and beating at me with his closed fists. I was fighting him off when I saw Rashida.

She was on the other side of the lattice, on the far side of the vegetable yard. She was carrying a tin, very carefully, but sometimes water dripped from it. She took it into the old toolshed.

"Look," I said. "Look, Lal. That's where her secret is." But he wouldn't look. He went on hitting me until I said that is must be something alive.

"To play with?" he said.

"Come on."

We were off then, the two of us, over the lattice gate (locked to keep the peacock in) and down to the shed. We yelled for Rashida, banged on the tin walls, and were answered by a kind of barking. We stayed still then and waited till she came out

She was very cross, but very worried. We must make no noise. No one must know.

"We want to see! We want to see!"

There was only one way to quiet us. She took us into the shed, over to a box where something moved in the half-light.

"A dog," cried Lal. "A puppy."

He was hushed into quiet. "You mustn't touch. It's sick. You mustn't make any noise. I've been nursing it for three days. You mustn't frighten it."

"Why don't you take it to Father?" Father could make everything well.

Rashida dropped her head. "He mustn't know." Lal and I looked at her. Secrets from Father!

"I went for the mail. I found it near the traps."

"Then it's a dingo puppy." Lal was fascinated. Dingoes were wild dogs, leapers at sheep. "But it's very little."

"We're not allowed near the traps!" I was the accuser. "Not even you. You'll get the strap."

"I know, I know."

"You won't get the mail any more." Rashida was the eldest, the one allowed to walk the four miles to the front gate and the mailbox.

"I know," Rashida was crying now, and Lal, from sympathy, sniffing. "It was crying. And its mother was dead in the trap. And there was blood ... I brought it home to wash. And now it's sick."

"It looks very sick. And its tail is bandaged."

"It was swelling."

"You'll have to take it to Father." I looked at her. "You'll be punished," I said.

"Yes," said Rashida. She wiped her eyes and then picked up the dog, fondling it.

"With the strap," I warned.

"Yes. But Father will make it well. I can't do any more."

We followed her, Lal and I, from the shed with the dog in her arms to the wash-house where the razor-strop hung. She put it over her shoulder and walked solemnly down the track to the fence where Father was mending. Lal and I went, too, following without a word. But when she handed Father the strap and stood there in front of him with the dog in her arms, Lal and I both burst into tears.

"What's this? What's this?"

"The strap," said Rashida.

He stood there, holding it awkwardly, looking at her while I cried and Lal kept saying, "Don't beat her, Father. Don't beat her."

"The dingo puppy is sick. You have to make it well," said Rashida. "I found it near the traps. You have to beat me."

Father burst out laughing, took the dog from Rashida's arms, and pulled off the bandage from its tail.

"It's a fox," he said. "All cubs have puffed-up tails. She is a vixen. She will have to have a lady's name."

"Kumari," I said, "because that means 'Princess'."

"Will she get well?" said Rashida.

Father laughed again. "Kumari will get well if you feed her with raw meat, if you give her water to drink, if you don't touch her food and don't touch her much. She's not used to the smell of wild little humans."

And so she was named, and her new life begun. She wore a red collar like Yasmin the goat, but without bells on it. She was fed on raw meat and kept from the chickens. And she grew. A handsome fox she was, but ours like a dog, to live with, to play with. She ran with us, ran to us with her strange, sharp barks and knelt to be patted. But she was Rashida's most of all, and they played the ball game together every evening after tea. Sometimes it was so dark that Rashida could not see, but still she threw the ball and as she stood there peering in the direction of its sound she would feel a soft nudging against her hand; Kumari had brought it back.

At night, at really-dark, at time for bed, Rashida used to take Kumari into the shed and watch her arrange herself in the box. Always she seemed happy there, but autumn came short days and longer nights. There was a bite in the air; we had great log fires. There was a stillness, a waiting about the nights.

It was then that Kumari began to whimper, to howl, to scratch at the shed door, to make a great banging noise as she flung herself at it. There was no playing now by day, only the whining, the rushing to the net fence and looking beyond it. She was sick again.

But Father would do nothing to make her well. Ama said we must wait. There was nothing to be done but watch. Rashida became sick with watching, too worried for food; she and Kumari were going to waste away together.

There was one night I remember, can remember even now, so long with the yelping and whining that in the morning Ama said that Kumari must go.

"Rashida," she said, "you must let her go. She is a grown thing now, and she wants to go away."

But Rashida would not hear. She said that Kumari was sick and would one day get better and be like a pet again, that she whined because she was sick and lonely in the shed away from Rashida, that she couldn't want to go away from the family that was her family.

"It is not her family," said Ama. "And she is grown now, what use is a family to her? When you are grown it will be time to go—from me, from all of us. It will be time to have a family of your own. It is time for Kumari, now."

"But she loves me, wants me, wants *me*," said Rashida.

"She is a fox, and she knows that now. She will never rest in a shed again. She wants the paddocks to run in, a hole to hide in."

"But she's safe here with me. She doesn't have to hide."

"She is a fox, and she knows it now. When she was small she did as you wanted, ran round like the dogs, but she knows now that we are not her kind and this is not her life. She is different from any animal you know. She does not belong on a farm."

"She's a nigger," I said.

Rashida began to cry.

"She is a stranger here," said Ama, "on her own. She is your responsibility, Rashida. You must decide; as though you were her mother, to let her go the way she has to. She is a fox. She will die if she stays here."

"She's mine," said Rashida. "She knows that I love her." And, calling Kumari, she ran out to the shed.

All day she sat there, fondling the stranger, whispering, pleading to her, but Kumari went on whimpering and trembling, refusing to eat or be comforted.

That night was the worst night of all with bark and whine and the banging on the shed door. I was almost asleep when I saw Rashida get out of bed.

"Where are you going?"

"I am going to let Kumari go."

I jumped out of bed and went with her. She lit the lantern and went into the yard. I was behind her, but I'm not sure that she knew, though she kept talking.

"I promised her," she was saying and she was crying, too. "I promised her tonight if she still wanted to go . . .

At the shed, it was I that cried. Rashida merely opened the door and held out her hand to Kumari.

"Come back," she was saying. "One day . . . ." But Kumari was gone, quicker than looking, through the door, over the fence and away.

"Stop crying," said Rashida. "She's gone now."

Later, in bed, she said suddenly, "Allah will watch over her."

"He is Lord of the high blue morning and the purple evening, the pink-rimmed sunset and the golden moon . . . ." I was remembering what Uncle Seyed had taught us. "The Koran doesn't say anything about foxes."

"It does," said Rashida. "All things belong to Him. In all things beautiful Allah smiles."

I didn't think Kumari beautiful, and I could see why you might call her a nigger, but I said nothing and hoped for Rashida's sake that she was right.

The next evening, Rashida took the ball out into the yard and played with it. She threw it and waited for Kumari suddenly to appear and bring it back. But always she had to get it herself, or send me or Lal. The next night she did the same. And the next ... But Lal and I were tired of playing at foxes and soon Rashida herself forgot the game.

One morning, at breakfast, we heard a squawking of fowls, and Father ran from the table. "That dog!" he was muttering.

But it was not a dog. We children, running behind him, had seen the red collar.

"Kumari," we called.

Kumari was dead.

"We have killed her," said Father. "I should not have let you keep her."

"I should not have let her go," said Rashida.

"She should have gone before. You see how thin she is... She had not learnt how to kill and hunt."

We could see the bones under her matted fur.

"There are scars."

"The other foxes did not want her now," said Father. "She had not their ways. She smelt of humans. There was no place for her."

"She loved us," said Rashida. "She was coming back to me."

"Only to die," said Father.

We buried her that morning, very solemnly, with the tennis-ball beside her and tears from Lal and me.

And that morning Father did not go out to work in the paddocks. He sat on the veranda with Ama and talked to her about India and watched us at our game.

MIRBANI

WHEN I was six I had a picnic.

Often we had picnics—tea from a billy, chuppatties from the house, games and laughing on the banks of the Gwydir— but I remember this one picnic because it was mine, not mother's or father's or uncle's or brother's or sister's, but mine for my birthday. I remember it also because of two presents that were wonderful then, and because the memory of one of them is wonderful even now.

There were birthday things to play with, especially for me, and birthday things to eat. But toys and food, these were real things to share and not the two things that were somehow mine.

It had been a dry time. Father and Uncle Seyed had fed the sheep by hand and carted water to the house, before the picnic. Now Father took me to walk with him by the river while the others prepared the birthday lunch. They all had jobs—Uncle Seyed, with Lal to help him, gathered wood to boil the billy; Ama our mother, and Rashida to help her, set out the meal. I had no job. It was my birthday. Father took my hand and we walked by the river.

I showed him all the things I knew, the secret things I never told Rashida, who was older than I was and told me I was little—the gum-tree where the wild bees made brown honey, the way you touched a trigger-plant and made it jump. And Father showed me things I should have seen, but, somehow, never had—the way the river was deep holes held together by shallow water, the way to stand still like a tree and see the fish move across the shallows.

We looked over to the hills where the river was born and suddenly Father laughed, his white teeth shining through his beard.

'I will give you a present," he said. "Not like Ama's present, but still a present. You see that cloud, the heavy one that's crawling over the hill, it will bring you rain for your birthday."

I knew that rain was wonderful, but I was greedy and wanted the other things. "What's Ama's present?"

"Ama's present is not now, not for now."

But later, when we all sat eating, when Uncle Seyed was in the middle of food and a long story about the old days and the old ways and the birthdays in the Punjab, Ama said, crossly for her, "Old days, old ways!"

Uncle Seyed stopped talking, even stopped eating for a moment. Then he went on, chewing thoughtfully, and looking sideways at Ama and wondering what was wrong.

"Nimmi," said Ama to me. "There is another present for you. Your grandmother is coming—my mother. All the way from India, a long way."

"She is a Brahmin," said Uncle Seyed. Then he bit at his chupatty like a fierce Muslim, as though he could eat all the Hindus in one bite.

"I was a Brahmin," said Ama.

"They don't eat meat," said little Lal. "I don't want a grandmother."

"She's my grandmother," I said. "Mine for my birthday." "How will she find us?" asked Rashida. "How will she know us when she sees us?"

"She is coming on a ship," said Father.

"I want to go on a ship," I said. "For my next birthday." "Greed!" said Father. "This birthday here and the next one wanted."

"Is India over the hills?" Lal pointed to them.

"Yes," said Ama, "a long way and across the water. Old days, and old ways. What will my mother think of us?"

"We can show her your garden," I said. "And the jasmine and the tamarisk will make her think that it's India."

"It is not India," said Father.

"And it is not the Punjab," said Uncle Seyed.

"It is just us," said Ama.

"Grandmother will like us." Lal sounded confident, but he ran to Ama and flung his arms round her. "Won't she?" he said. "Won't she?"

"Yes, yes," said Ama. "But now we must go home. Lal must be home and warm before the rain comes."

We hurried to pack everything into the wagon, everyone hurried. Lal had only to be tired and we were frightened. He was the only boy we had, and he was sickly and was sometimes pale. On the way home Rashida and I took turns at nursing the baby, but Ama held Lal all the way home because he was shivering.

That night it rained. The rain fell on the roof with a great noise that frightened me, and I woke Rashida. She laughed at me and then talked until the rain was falling soft and always like a quali song and we fell asleep again.

In the morning Ama told us that Lal was sick, that he had to stay in bed, that if we talked to him we must be quiet, that we were not to make him quick and impatient. But we could not have done that. Even when we made jokes for him he hardly smiled. When I brought Sulieman the rooster in to see him he only stretched his hand out to him so slowly and so tired—as if the bird was a long way away. He didn't even try to pull its tail and Rashida and I knew that he was sick, and though we smiled we were frightened. In a few days he was more sick than we could remember.

The doctor came from town, in his car, and Rashida and I waved to him because we knew him. When he was going he drove us to the gate with him so that we could open it and swing on it and when he had gone through we could wave to him again.

"You must be very kind to Lal," he said, "and quiet. It is not a cold. It is not his asthma. It is not anything I know yet. We have to wait and see. This is your secret, you two. You must not tell the others that we don't know. We will wait and see and be kind to him, and when we know what is wrong with him we will make him well."

Grandmother came—she also was in a car. If Lal had been well he would have said that was wrong, she should have come in a ship. But not even Grandmother could bring a ship along a road.

She came in the night when we were sleeping and in the morning, when we knew that she had come, we were afraid —Rashida and I—and felt very small. Ama had told us things about her that had made her seem very clever and certain, very grown-up. Ama, as she told us, seemed a little bit frightened and not at all grown-up and sure the way we had always thought of her; Ama seemed like us.

"What will she think of us?" she said. "What will she think of me?"

She told us how Grandmother was Hindu and not Muslim, had never known Allah; How she was Brahmin and her family was Brahmin and did not eat the food we ate, did not talk to the people we talked to. She told us how strong Grandmother was, so strong and sure that she had not done what her parents said was right but had left them and had married a bad Brahmin who talked to everyone and did work that he should not have done; so clever that after she was married she had gone to school and had learnt English and Hindi and Tamil and other languages, and she could read them now— even the most ancient Hindu writings. She had had a newspaper of her own and had been in prison. She had worked hard and now that she was old her children did the work that she had done. They taught, and wrote and made speeches. They worked for the Government and were very clever and very good. All of them were clever, all except Ama—our mother.

Ama was not clever. She had listened while the others read. She was the eldest and she minded the young ones.

She was shy and she would not go out, not even to school. Grandmother told her she was a child, the eldest and a child, a girl who would never be a woman. Sometimes Ama used to cry and want to be like the others in her family.

One day, Grandfather brought a Muslim to the house. He spoke no Hindi. The talk was in English, which Ama knew, and she listened to him. He talked of his farm in New England, in Australia. He told how the paddocks were big as villages and the hills were not high enough for snow. He described strange animals and he helped his funny English with his hands. He showed how kangaroos moved, and possums. He tried to sing like a strange bird, which he said was "best than flutes in India". He said there were birds that laughed, and he smiled with white teeth at Ama's listening.

Often he came when there was no one in the house to listen, only Ama. Grandfather and Grandmother were busy. The children were busy. There were things to be done. But always Ama was there to listen and one day, when he said that it was the last time he would come, he asked Ama to marry him.

"Oh, how Grandmother shouted!" said Ama. "How she cried out! She said he was a Muslim, and black. He could not read or write. He had left his country and run away. He had done nothing for his people and everything for himself. He wanted to take me where there was no one to be friends. I would be lonely. Oh, how she argued! Then, I became a Muslim."

This was terrible. Even Grandfather, who was a bad Brahmin, was upset.

"The Gods will punish," he said. "The Gods will punish."

And they did—as they always do. Grandmother wrote to Ama and told her Grandfather was dead. Ama's baby, her first-born, her boy, opened his eyes to die, and the farm and the hills and the birds and the animals were all strange and not here. And she was as lonely as if the whole world was not here.

"Once," she told us, "your father brought me a rabbit to cook and then went out to work on the farm. And I sat there alone, near the window with all the strange world watching me. I cried and cried and plucked the rabbit, every bit of fur. I had never seen a rabbit before. And then you came, Rashida. And then you, Nimmi. And then Lal, our boy. And then Jamila, the baby. I have been very happy, but Mother—your grandmother—this has been a lonely time for her. She has made her house like a hospital, full of people, but not one of her own. Her children are all of them away, working, being clever and good, and not with her. And what will she think of me? She will think I am nothing, eh?" Ama laughed then as though she were joking, but she was not.

"I don't want to see any old grandmother," I told Rashida.

But in the kitchen, in the morning, when we knew that she had come, we called out and questioned and wanted to see her.

Uncle Seyed laughed at us. "You will not be so happy when we sit down to dinner with her. There will be no meat in the house."

"But we have meat every day!"

"It would not be polite," said Uncle Seyed, shocked at our manners. "Your grandmother is a wretch of a Brahmin. It would not be right to have meat in the house."

"What else is there to eat?"

"Dal," said Uncle Seyed.

We thought about dal, curry made from peas and lentils, and we looked miserable enough to please even Uncle Seyed. He smiled at us.

"I am lucky," he said. "I can cook for myself down in my own house, but your poor father—your poor father! I suppose I could give you some meat if you were good."

"I don't mind eating dal," said Rashida. She was always telling lies and trying to be grown-up.

"I hate dal," I said. "And so does Rashida."

When Ama came into the kitchen she made us all go away. "You must be quiet," she said. "Grandmother has come a long way. She is tired."

In the garden, Rashida and I talked about her and wondered if she were very old. "She is over sixty," said Rashida. "She is terribly, terribly old."

We thought about terribly old people for a little while, but by the time Ama called us to the house we had forgotten about the old people of the world and were playing and fighting the way that we always did.

We ran to the house and then, shy, we followed Ama inside. Suddenly, from surprise or from shyness we stood still and heard a voice saying in Hindi, Ama's language, "*my* granddaughters. My Australian granddaughters."

It was not only the voice that was beautiful. The gold threads of her sari glittered in the sunlight that shone through the window, and her face was not old the way we meant old, though her hair was grey at the sides, like white wings. On her forehead was the round blue mark of the Brahmins and her eyes—big and kind and dark like Ama's—looked at us. She was very small. Her long gold ear-rings and her heavy bangles looked like chains, even though they were pretty. She was calling our names. "Rashida. Nimmi."

I dropped my eyes and saw how small her feet were in their gold-cord sandals. I turned and hid my face in Ama's dress, but she pulled me round to face her mother. "This is your nani, your grandmother," she said. "Be friends."

"I have brought thee presents," said the stranger in her sweet Hindi.

"Presents?" said Rashida.

"I will give them to thee." She opened a box that was on the table. It was full of parcels. There was one that had to be taken in to the bedroom, to Lal—a sulwa and a jacket of white silk, a hat with gold thread on it and slippers that turned up at the toes. There was a parcel for the baby—tiny gold bangles, and gold ear-rings for when she was big. There was a parcel for

Rashida and me, "the impatient ones" as Grandmother laughed and called us—bangles and ear-rings, and silver ankle-chains with tiny bells to ring wherever you walked. We put them on and made Ama laugh at the way we ran and skipped and jumped, to make music.

But the present that was for Ama made her cry. It was a pair of long gold ear-rings and the part that hung was a lotus flower of little rubies and pearls. Ama held them in her hand.

"They are Kashmir," she said. "They are home, and the flowers at home."

We danced then to cheer her and our feet made silvery sounds as the sun jangled on our chains. We all laughed and smiled.

Then we showed our nani, our grandmother, everything— the Indian garden, the gum-trees and the kurrajongs, Jasmin the goat and Shah-Jehan the peacock. We explained the hills—their names and how there were only five of them— and all the work on the farm. We pointed to magpies and kookaburras. And, in the days after, we followed her like shadows, like slaves, talking in Hindi and calling each other "thou" and trying to speak beautifully, like her. Even when she sat quietly by Lal's bed, whispering him stories that we thought were stories for babies, we stayed close to her and listened. Because we loved her.

And we loved her food, too. The dal she cooked was wonderful, full of spices and strange tastes. She made other curries, from eggs and from all sorts of vegetables that we had never thought were vegetables at all. We tried to learn how to make them, too.

Sometimes, though, after sitting politely through our Brahmin dinners, Father would go from the house and visit Uncle Seyed, who was eating meat like a virtuous Muslim.

The day we visited Uncle Seyed's house he was not at home, and before we took Grandmother in to see the furniture he had made Rashida ran ahead and hid his meat-safe in the wood-shed. If Grandmother had known she would most probably have laughed—unless she was as polite as we were being.

Lal became very ill. Uncle Seyed rode into town to bring the doctor and Grandmother, no longer playing tired, gracious and kind, became the hospital-lady—bathing Lal's head, darkening his room, and telling all of us what we must do, even Ama and Father and Uncle Seyed. It was she who ordered Uncle to ride for the doctor, and he went.

When the doctor came he said it was meningitis, and the long strange word made Ama afraid. But Grandmother simply asked him what was to be done, and she wrote down all that he said.

Lal lay on the bed and did not know us, not one of us. Sometimes he called out the names of his birds and his voice sounded like Lal. But sometimes there was no sound except his breathing, thick and whispering, not like Lal at all.

Every day Grandmother sat by his bed and every day the doctor came from town. Whenever Ama was free of the kitchen and the baby she sat with Grandmother, the two of them watching the boy.

One morning when Grandmother sat in the garden, very tired and quiet, with her eyes shut, I ran up to her—to talk. I was lonely. Rashida had no time for me; she was being grown-up and helping—helping in the kitchen, helping with the baby—so that Ama could be with Lal. So I called Grandmother "Nani" and started to chatter. She opened her eyes and looked at me. She leant against the wall and looked at me. She seemed suddenly very old, very tired.

"Punjabi voices," she said. "Punjabi faces. There is nothing of my people in my children here."

I wanted to be a Punjabi like Father—I always had—but I wanted to please Grandmother and I would have liked to be like her and like Ama, too. Suddenly I had a thought.

"Mirbani," I said.

"Mirbani" is a Hindi word. There is no word in Punjabi like it, and there is none in English unless it is grace, the state of grace, or graciousness. It is a word that means all those things, and something more.

"What, child? What?"

"That is you, Nani," I said. "Mirbani."

Grandmother began to laugh. "I was wrong," she said. "There is the soul of the Brahmin in thee. Thou knowest how to flatter and to please. Thou knowest the words that should be true." She held me to her and talked to me, or to herself, or to God. "My daughter threw away the Hindu in her, but she has paid for that. Her first-born, her son of sons, is dead. But this one, little Lal, must live. There has to be an end to punishment, even God cannot be always cruel. This one has to live."

Then, for the first time, I really knew how very sick Lal was. Later that day, I knew it again. The doctor had gone. Father and Uncle Seyed were talking on the verandah. "The doctor is a good man," I heard Father say, "kind, but he says tomorrow we will know. Lal must be better in the morning, or Lal will die."

"He is a good man," said Uncle Seyed, "but he is only a man. Lal will get well. Allah is kind. Remember. Remember that first year, the black year, the drought and the sheep dying—we prayed to Him then, and He did help us. And when first I came to this country, and knew no one, how I prayed that I might find my friend and how my path led—somehow—here. We must pray now. You must have faith."

"The first son died," said Father. "I cannot hope, I dare not hope. I cannot pray, I cannot be weak. I have to be strong—to bear this one's going."

"I will pray," said Uncle Seyed. "I will pray all night."

I was like Father. I could not pray either. Is it true? I thought. Could Lal die? Allah is good. Uncle Seyed is always saying that, Allah is good. But Allah belongs to the Punjab. He is a long way—a long way from home and me and Lal.

I went into Ama's garden, her Indian world, and I looked out through the squares in the lattice at paddock and sky, at the five hills that were our hills. Ama gave them to each of us when we were born. As soon as she was well she carried each new one, each Australian, out through the garden with its Indian jasmine and Kashmiri roses and Himalayan violets and out through the lattice-gate where all the Australian world was watching. She held each of us up so that we would see the hills and she told them, and all the Gods that were, that we had come. "This is Nimmi," she had said when she held me. "Nimmi whom the Gods must love."

"Oh, love *him*! Love Lal!" I cried out, whimpered and prayed. "He's little and gets frightened. He thinks Kashmir is over the hills and ships sail on the land. He doesn't know anything. Love him and keep him safe. Keep him with us, so I can teach him things."

But that night—late, late—when morning should have come, another came. Like a snake, like a cobra—silent and not to be seen—it came inside our house; it passed Uncle Seyed with his prayer-mat, his Koran and his strange droning song, passed the room where I was sleeping, passed Rashida, passed the baby and the cradle that Father had made, passed Father and Ama and their worried sleep. It did not wake them. It was not for them or for me or for the others that it had come. It was for Lal.

It went into his room, but there was a woman there—her eyes heavy-lidded but her mind and all of her waiting, as the stranger knew. She was the old enemy. She was the watching one. It was she who had hated him in his rages of famine and cholera, who had fought to bar his way. And even now, silent as he was and still as death, she knew that he was there. She flung aside the wet cloth she had used to cool Lal's forehead. She stood up to him—small, her sari glittering—and suddenly she fell down by the bed, as though the stranger had beaten her. But she fell only to kneel, and her hands held Lal as though she would not let him go. "Ram! Ram!" she prayed. "Save this Thy reed that is shaken by the wind. Save this Thy son. Let him not yet enter the house of clay… "

Outside, Uncle Seyed called on Allah, the All-merciful, the Compassionate…

Then—as Grandmother, Nani, Mirbani explained it—the God of the Brahmins looked on her frailty and faith and the God of the Muslims looked on His stubborn praying son and the two of them together, two Gods in one, drove out the stranger, out from the house, the garden, the paddocks, over the hills, and beyond our world.

Uncle Seyed explained it differently. "I told you," he said. "Didn't I tell you that Allah would make him well again?"

The doctor smiled, and it seemed then that the whole world smiled—that spring was really spring. Every day Lal grew more like Lal and life in the house became what it had always been. Father and Uncle Seyed went working in the paddocks. Ama fussed over the house, and Grandmother Mirbani was a guest again and not a nurse. She sat with us —Rashida and me—and talked of the old days, the old ways. Wonderful stories she told us, and Lal, now he was allowed to walk, followed her like a shadow—"Like my son," she laughed.

Then the car came to take her from us, to take her the long way. We cried, of course, and she talked and talked to stop us, said she would send us presents, messages in her letters to Ama, that she would come back some day and we would all laugh because we had cried. But when she lifted Lal up in her arms, her eyes were tearful and she whispered in Hindi, "Alas, I will never see thee again." She put him down quickly and smiled at us.

Uncle Seyed spoke. He spoke in Hindi, a language he disapproved of; it was the greatest compliment he could pay.

"I thank thee," he said, "for the life of the little one who is like my own, for thy nursing, for—thy prayers. Yes," he said bravely, "for thy prayers. I know that it was thou who turned death from him and I will thank thee with all my life. I will pray Allah that He watch over thee and bless thy days."

"What words!" said Mirbani. "What words! Thou art my children's friend, thou art my son. There can be no talk of thanks. But I do thank thee—for *thy* prayers."

"I will still eat meat, though!" said Uncle Seyed.

Mirbani laughed. We all laughed — longer than we needed. It was to a sound like laughter that Mirbani drove away.

THE OUTLAWS

THE stories that Ama our mother told us were gentle and strange, stories of the time when magic people walked through Hindustan, and everything they touched was right and good.

Father's stories were true and real; how he had moved through Australia as a hawker and how at night he turned from the southern stars to pray towards Mecca, how he was a boy in the Punjab and how he had found Uncle Seyed…

Uncle Seyed! His stories were different—not always gentle, not always real—but somehow, sometimes, we believed them and remembered them as we remembered nothing else. Perhaps it was because he told us so few, he was shy with us. Perhaps it was because his stories were for grown-ups, he was the one who made Father laugh. But his story of the outlaws was a story only for me, and I remember it.

The day I heard it was a day like any day. That's how it started.

It was a hot day, it was summer; it was the farm, there were jobs to be done. Father was in the paddock with the sheep. My sister Rashida and I were helping Ama in the kitchen. The smell of spice was everywhere; Ama was making curry. She was roasting the seeds of cumin, coriander, black pepper. She was softening them for the grinding, when they could be blended with clove, cardamon, chilli, cinnamon, and mace.

Rashida was cutting mangoes and lemons into quarters, ready to be turned into chutney. I was too young to be allowed a knife and I sat at the table by her and stalked the chillies, so that they could be salted and set in trays on the roof, to dry in the sun.

The sun was everywhere in the kitchen, in Rashida's singing and in the rows of new-washed bottles that were waiting for Ama's curry powder. They sparkled so that I watched them and suddenly, when the sun moved, they dazzled me so that I put my hand to my eyes.

My eyes began to stab at me, and I cried out with pain.

"What is it? What is it, Nimmi?" Ama dropped her pan of seeds and ran to hold me while I cried. Rashida laughed.

"Stupid!" she said. "She had chilli on her hand and she rubbed it in her eyes. She's too young to be in the kitchen." She went on cutting mangoes and looking grown-up.

Ama frowned at her, told me not to cry, and got the earthen jug of water to bathe my eyes.

The water was cool and healing. The pain grew less, but I leant hard against Ama and whimpered; it was not often I was given so much attention. Rashida looked envious.

Ama washed my hands. "Rashida and I will finish this," she said. "You go into the garden. Play with Lal and baby."

Rashida chopped away and smiled at me as though she were grown up. Not happily I went into the garden.

Lal was there, putting stones round a flower-bed. "Always making yourself dirty!" I said to him.

The baby was in her pram, under the jasmine vine. She was kicking her naked feet and laughing. I waggled a finger at her. She caught it and put it in her mouth, but I pulled it away sternly.

"You're too young," I said. "You're too young and stupid to know about chilli. You are lucky, Jamila, that I washed it off."

I looked at my finger. "You've got a tooth," I said. "You've got a tooth!" I opened her mouth. There were two —two white bumps. "Lal!" I shouted. "Jamila has a tooth! Two teeth! Come and see."

Lal came running with his spade and his dirty hands. He grasped the side of the pram and pulled himself up on to his toes so that he could see.

"Show me," he said.

I opened her mouth.

"Oh, the clever baby!" said Lal. "The clever baby!"

I laughed and ran towards the kitchen. Rashida was washing her hands at the tank.

"Jamila has teeth. Come and see."

I ran back to the pram and Rashida followed me. Even she ran. I pulled open the baby's mouth to show her, but this time baby objected; it was no longer a game. She screamed.

"Oh, hush, hush!" I said to her. "Don't let Ama hear. Ama will hate us if you cry."

Rashida rocked the pram the way that Ama did. "Little dove," she pleaded, just like Ama, "little rose-petal, hush!" But the little rose-petal screwed up its face and screamed more fiercely than before.

"What wrong?" said a voice. "What wrong?" It was Uncle Seyed come into the garden.

"She cries," said Rashida. "All the time, she cries." She rocked the pram so frantically that Uncle Seyed laughed. He took charge then, the way he always did when he thought we were funny.

"Not that way," he said. "That not the way. I show you." He rocked the pram gently, very gently, and leant over the baby. She looked up at him, and stopped for a breath. He grabbed her then and lifted her from the pram, held her up so quickly and so high that she laughed. Then he carried her round the garden, rocking her, playing with her, lifting her to see things and singing all the time the way that he and Father sang—not the gentle or the gay songs of Ama and Rashida, but the quali songs of the Punjab, the high-pitched wailing that the baby loved. She even stopped laughing. She gazed at him with awe. He put her back in the pram. "She likes singing," he said. "That the way."

"I don't like quali," I said. "It sounds like dingoes."

"Why you no speak English?" said Uncle Seyed. He always spoke English to us, his sort of English. "Your father speak Punjabi all time and he speak not English. You speak English all time and you speak good English, like me."

I looked at him and tried not to laugh. The trying must have made me look sad because when Rashida went back to the kitchen he said to me, "You get hat and ask Ama can you come with me. I going to fix fence near Out-law's Cave. Not hard job. We can talk. We can talk English."

"Me!" said Lal. "Can I come, too?"

Uncle Seyed looked at little Lal. "We ask Ama," he said.

Ama put my hat on for me and shook her head to Uncle Seyed when he pointed to Lal.

"Lal-baba," said Uncle Seyed, "your father is in paddock. I must mend fence. What man stay to look after Ama, Rashida, the baby?"

"I am afraid," said Ama, "when there is no man here."

Lal looked at her and her downcast head. He looked at Uncle Seyed. "I must stay," he said. "Men must look after women."

So Uncle Seyed and I went alone to the Outlaw's Cave, and the story that day was given to me.

We went on Saladin, the blue horse that only Uncle Seyed could ride. But he was quiet with both of us on him, and he galloped beautifully while Uncle Seyed sang.

The cave was on the boundary fence and when we got there Uncle Seyed tethered Saladin in the shade of a big gum-tree. He patted him and talked to him gently for a long time.

"You don't speak to him in English," I said, but I said it so softly that neither Uncle Seyed nor Saladin heard.

I walked over to the cave. It was big; Uncle Seyed could have stood up inside. It was long, too; Saladin could have sheltered in it from the rain and have not been seen from outside. I walked round it and felt the walls until I was bored. I went out into the light again and watched Uncle Seyed working on the fence, fixing the wires.

"Uncle Seyed," I said. "Why is it called the Outlaw's Cave?"

Uncle Seyed hammered at a post. "In old days an outlaw live here," he said. "A bushranger."

"Bushranger?"

"We say 'dacoit'. In Australia say 'bushranger'."

"What was his name?"

"Thunderbolt," said Uncle Seyed. "His name Thunderbolt."

I had heard that name, and I repeated it excitedly.

"Real name Ward," said Uncle Seyed. "He steal horses— good horses. But not good like Saladin. He hide here and policeman not catch him. My word, he hard man to catch!"

"But they caught him?"

"They kill him," said Uncle Seyed. "They shoot him in water. He have no chance. Grave in Uralla. I show you one day."

I gaped at the cave. "But he was a bad man," I said.

"People here like him, sorry he killed. I sorry. He like horses."

I stared at him. Uncle Seyed was devout and embarrassingly honest. "But he was a thief," I said.

Uncle Seyed stopped banging the post. "Are thieves that are thieves," he said. "Are thieves that are men. Some men steal and die, but they not crawl street with begging-bowl. Better to steal and die. A man ... a man can be a thief," he said. Without noticing, he had begun to speak in Punjabi. "A man can steal and still have honour. He can be a great dacoit, great. Like Malik Khan."

"Who was Malik Khan?" I said very softly, in Punjabi, and I sat down near him because I knew that a story was coming.

Uncle Seyed did not even look at me. He fixed his eyes on the hills and stared as though he saw other hills and not the ones that he knew and all of us knew every day of our lives.

He looked at the hills and told me, for my own, the story of Malik Khan.

I was not born in your father's village, I came there in my twelfth year. I came there from Peshawar where I was born. I lived in Peshawar until I was twelve, older than Rashida.

At that time in Peshawar there were soldiers everywhere, the frontier was alive with killing; it was the place where Malik Khan lived. He was the eagle that struck from the mountains. He was the great dacoit.

There was money to be had for him—from the British, from the rich Indians. There was money to be had for those who could catch him, kill him, bring him back. But no one asked for that money, for no one who knew him would betray him. Who would betray an eagle?

I was small and often I thought of him. I would sit in the doorway with the Mullah, my Koran teacher, and not listen. The Mullah was an old man with grey hair, very wise and strangely brave; Muslims saluted when he passed them, even the British respected him, but a small boy thinking of a fierce man like an eagle used to sit by him and let him talk and not listen. I used to watch the people in the street and wonder if some of them — the tall fair-skinned ones, the Pathans—were not men from Malik Khan's camp. If one of them might not have been Malik Khan himself.

I watched them come in to pray, watched them pick flowers in the garden, watched them put the flowers in their hair. Flowers are precious to Pathans. There are no flowers in the hills that they call home; there are no flowers where a Malik Khan must hide.

I was watching the flower-pickers and wondering when, suddenly, the Mullah said something that I heard.

"My teacher," I said to him. "My teacher, how can you? How can you go to Malik Khan? Even the soldiers cannot find him out, and they have guns and they look every day, How can you?"

The Mullah smiled. He disapproved of the British soldiers; they threw their bottles in the holy garden.

"Soldiers!" he said. "Guns!" Talk but no manners. Power, but no sense. They do not know our people. I know our people. I know them a little."

I stared at him and thought about it: that much was true.

He had observed two Pathans that he had marked for Malik Khan's and, on the day that he was ready, he followed them. In his teacher's robes, in the green turban that showed he had been to Mecca, he followed them. He knew they would hesitate to shoot at such a man.

He followed them out of Peshawar, along the dusty road until they came to the Khyber Road where—suddenly, in a lonely pass—the Pathans wheeled their horses and waited for him.

"I have no money," he told them. "You cannot rob me. I have no gun; I cannot shoot you. I am a Mullah who has been to Mecca and who wishes to speak with your chief."

They pretended not to understand, asked him what chief, swore they were travellers and not thieves, told him to go quickly on his way because the hills were dangerous.

The Mullah listened to all that they said, but as every sentence finished he asked for Malik Khan, and when all the sentences were finished and the men had turned their horses to leave him he demanded from them in a loud clear voice *nanawatai, melastia, badragga*.

The Pathans stopped and looked at him, dismayed. These words—sanctuary, hospitality, safe-conduct—are part of the law of the Pathans. A man who breaks them, a man who refuses them, is no Pathan and all his people are dishonoured.

Dismayed, they looked at him, saw his horse ready to follow them, his helplessness if they attacked him, his humble white robes and his proud green turban. They cursed him as they granted what he had asked.

They bound his eyes and took him blindly to the outlaw's hide-out. When they undid the cloth the Mullah's open eyes saw Malik Khan himself.

"Malik Khan," said the Mullah. "Malik Khan, my son. I taught you the Koran. I knew you as a boy. Your teacher asks, commands, that you become the man that boy should be and never a dacoit."

The outlaw smiled. "My father," he said, "it is not possible."

"You loot. You steal. You are hunted like a wolf. Like a wolf you will be caught. The soldiers must find you. One day the guns must speak. You know that you must die."

Malik Khan stared at him. "It is true," he said. "It is true, my father, but come with me. Father, come with me."

He took the Mullah to a high rock from which they could see the road that wound from the valley to the frontier.

"There," he said. "There on that road, day after day, come caravans of wealth—wealth that can be taken in a single raid. Silk from Bokhara, gold from Peshawar, food." He turned the Mullah's head gently to gaze up at the hills, the tribal land of the Pathans. "There," he said. "There!"

The Mullah looked up and saw the hills steep and barren, rock and dust, thorn and scrub, the hills that grew into the mountains between the Khyber and Afghanistan, the hills so bare that they held no water.

"A hole in the ground to catch some water," said Malik Khan. "A cave in the rock to be a house. It is necessary to steal. It is necessary to kill. It is necessary to be hunted like a wolf. If the children hunger, are we to let them starve?"

"It is not right," said the Mullah. "It is not good."

He turned to speak to the others. They were Muslims, devout and yet dacoit. They would go to jail rather than swear false oaths, but they would kill if they had to kill to eat. He spoke to them of the Koran and of Allah's blessing of life, but there was nothing he could say to them and he felt very old and foolish. "There is nothing I can say to you, my sons."

Malik Khan held him by the shoulders. "Father," he said, "be content. This is the life we were born into. This is the life we are given. Go to your home in Peshawar, and be content."

It was night when the Mullah left. His eyes were unbound and Malik Khan himself came to be his guide. They moved between the rocks towards the place where the Mullah's horse had been hidden and the Mullah's robes glowed white in the moon's light.

A guard on the hillside, one of Malik's men, raised his gun to fire at the white-robed stranger.

Too late Malik saw the gleam of the barrel. Too late he called. But he flung himself in front of the Mullah and the bullet went into him.

"*Nanawatai, melmastia, badragga*," said Malik Khan before he died.

The Mullah and the weeping guard took the body back to its family and its people. For three days the Mullah stayed with them—helping, comforting—and then he came back to the town where I was, a small boy who did not listen, and he told us all that the great dacoit was dead.

The great merchants threw food to the people, so that even the poor would rejoice, and the soldiers drank beer and sang. And some of them threw their bottles into the masjid garden where the Mullah sat grieving as though he had lost a son.

And I grieved, too, as though I had lost something great. And the next year I came to your father's village and found you all.

Uncle Seyed looked at me suddenly and smiled.

"I found you, eh?" he said in English.

I nodded, but said nothing. I was trying hard to remember the two stories, Thunderbolt and Malik Khan, to lock them safe in my head for afterwards, the two outlaws who touched my life.

When we rode home the smell of curry found us and Uncle Seyed laughed again.

"We live and we eat," he said in Punjabi. "It is good to live in Australia."

"We live and we eat," I said to him in English.

"Is good?" said Uncle Seyed, remembering. "Is good," said Uncle Seyed in his sort of English, "to speak English like me?"

HIGH MAHARAJAH

SUMMER was done. The sky that had been white with heat was blue. The days that had been long and heavy were short and gentle. All day now we could have flown our kites.

We flew them in the afternoons in the big paddock that had been cleared for the horses. There was no scrub there to trip us as we ran, no trees to trap or tear the kites.

My kite, like Lal's, was home-made. Its face was newspaper—brown paper was too heavy—but when it was swaying in the sky it looked grey and beautiful. But it was the tail that was really beautiful. It was red and green cloth that Ama had dyed especially to be beautiful.

Rashida's kite was different. It sang. It had come from India. When Rashida was born an old friend of Father's had sent it to him, for her. It had been bright green when she had first flown it, but that was a long time ago and it had had many coloured faces since then. But the sticks and the pierced bamboo reed that was the kite's voice, they were always the same.

The coloured paper to make its faces came from Song Ling, a Chinaman who had a store in town. Sometimes his goods were packed in coloured paper and he always saved it for us. A long time ago, in China, he had flown kites, too. Father kept the paper in a box. It was used only for Rashida's kite, which we all knew was special; it could sing.

We wound the kite strings round bamboo rollers which Father had brought with him from the Punjab. He had been the best kite-flyer in his village. He used to tell us stories of the kite seasons there and of the Basant Panchami, the spring festival, when all India flew kites and there were competitions to see who flew them best.

Ama told us stories, too, legends about brave young rajahs using kites as messengers of love, of a general who cheered his soldiers by tying a lantern to a kite and telling them it was the star of victory, of villagers who all night long flew singing kites so that they might sing away every harm and hurt.

But these things belonged to India and legend and not to Rashida, not to Lal and not to me. We flew our kites because we loved the dip and dive and sway of them against the sky, the tug of the string on the rollers in our hands. That was why we took the billy of flour-and-water paste, the paper for mending, the string and our kites down to the big paddock and chased the horses away from us, down to the far end where the trees were.

"Rashida," I said, "there is no string for your kite."

She looked at the rollers. "I'll use ordinary string."

"Your kite's too big. Father said you had to use the thick string."

"It will be all right," said Rashida. "The wind is not strong today."

We were tying the string to the kites when Lal mentioned the High Maharajah. We looked up at the sky, looked in every direction.

"He is not here," said Rashida.

"He always comes when we fly our kites," I said.

"We can't fly them unless we ask him," said Lal, looking as though he would cry. "He is the king of the sky."

"We can't ask him," said Rashida, "if he's not here."

We stared at the third hill. It was from there that he always came.

"Perhaps he can see us," I said, "even if we can't see him."

"But we have to ask," said Lal. "We always ask him first."

"I suppose we could salaam," said Rashida. "That should satisfy him." But it was Lal she was thinking about, not the High Maharajah.

We bowed very low towards the third hill. Then Rashida began grabbing at the kites.

We put Lal's kite up first; he was little and always needed help. Then Rashida and I put mine up; sometimes I needed help, too. Then Rashida put her own up; she was bigger than we were and she never needed help.

The kites flew high, riding the wind. The newspaper kites danced and Rashida's bright orange kite sang for them, sang for us, sang for the whole world. The string spun on the rollers, playing out and out, while the kites danced higher. They were pulling at our hands and arms and we were running with them. It was as though we were flying and dancing, too.

Suddenly Lal gave a shout. "Look! The High Maharajah!"

And there he was—the High Maharajah of the Sky, the great eagle that owned the air. Serenely and without haste he circled the three kites. His wings hardly moved. He glided solemnly while they danced for him and Rashida's kite sang. And then, as if approving, he soared suddenly high— higher than all the kites in the world. He circled once more, looking at us, and then flew towards the third hill.

"He is beautiful," said Rashida.

"He is too big," I said. "I am glad he doesn't come close to us."

"He is the High Maharajah," said Lal. "He would never hurt us."

"I want to fly," said Rashida, and she jumped up and down with her kite as though she were flying already. "If I could fly I would go so far, so far up, that no kite could catch me. I'd be so high that you, Nimmi, and you, Lal, would look like ants—would look smaller than ants. I would fly up so high that I could see all the world, everything, the whole world spread out like a carpet." She flung out her arms, to show us how wide the world was. The roller fell from her hand and her kite began to leap away.

I screamed and Lal shouted and Rashida grabbed desperately to catch the string. It was cutting her hand, but she held on to it. With my free hand, I tried to pick up her roller. I had just got it when Rashida jerked the string—to make it hurt less — and it snapped. It snapped high up, farther than Rashida could jump, farther than we could reach. We could only stand—Lal and I with our newspaper kites and Rashida with her useless string—and watch the singing kite fly upwards and away from us like a bird that had been set free.

At home, Ama scolded Rashida and called her impatient. She sat disconsolate.

"No tears," said Father. "I will write to India. We will get another singing kite."

"It will not be the same," said Rashida. "It will not be mine for being born."

We were out searching for it when we saw Mr Angus. He was our neighbour, a big man with a voice so loud it frightened you, but with so many smiles that that didn't matter.

"Oh, Mr Angus!" said Rashida. "Have you seen an orange kite?"

"No kites today," he said. "Not even orange ones." Suddenly he looked up at the sky. "There's that eaglehawk again. Savage-looking brute."

"It's the High Maharajah," I said. "He wouldn't harm a fly."

"Not thinking of flies," said Mr Angus. "Thinking of your father's lambs. I'll shoot him if he comes near my place."

"You couldn't shoot him!" We were shocked.

"You're right," he said. "I couldn't shoot him. Too quick, too mean, too cunning."

I looked at his gun. "But if you see him again—"

"I'll raise my hat to him."

The next day Mr Angus came to our place. He had brought some things from town that Father wanted on the farm.

"That kite," he said, "did you find it?"

"No," said Rashida. "We will never find it."

"Then you'd better look at these." He handed her a long thin parcel. "I'll take them back, if you don't like them." "Kites!" said Rashida. "Australian kites!"

There were three of them — one pink, one green, one orange. Father and Mr Angus put the sticks together and fitted the faces over them. They were big kites, as tall as Lal, and the orange one was for Rashida.

But when we were running down to the paddock to fly them Rashida said, "It is not the same. There is no kite in Australia that can sing."

"What is the Maharajah doing?" said Lal.

He was there, at the foot of the third hill, flying low over the bush and scrub. Sometimes he swooped down out of sight. We watched and saw him do it many times. He would hover over the one place, circling and dipping, then he would fall towards the ground. He was like a kite that would not stay up.

"There must be something wrong with him," said Rashida. "He must be hurt. Lal, you mind the kites. Nimmi and I are going to see what's the matter with him."

"I'm not going," I said. "He's too big. We should go and get Father."

"We won't go close," said Rashida. "Just close enough to see if he is hurt."

I followed her then, as I always did.

The Maharajah had not risen for a long time, but we walked towards the scrub around which he had hovered. The track was overgrown. It was rocky and the trees grew low to the ground.

"We should go back now. He must have flown away."

"Just a little bit further." Rashida kept saying that.

At last she leant against a big rock. "We'll go back now," she said, "He is nowhere here."

Suddenly there was a noise from the other side of the rock. There was a movement of branches and a sound like a rushing wind. We looked up and saw red eyes, hooked beak and huge red-brown feathered body. The wings were beating over our heads and the great bird was very close.

We clung to each other, hiding our eyes, terrified. But we could not hide our ears. The beating of those mighty wings became the beating of our own hearts.

When Rashida realized that, she raised her head and made me raise mine. High, high in the blue was the Maharajah, a speck, a tiny thing moving towards his hill.

Rashida went round to the other side of the rock and then called me to her. "Look!"

It was the singing kite. Its tail was caught in a bush. It was moving in the wind, bumping up and down. The sticks were broken. The orange face was dashed to pieces, but the bamboo reed—the voice, the singer, the kite's own self—was safe.

Ama scolded us at home. "You are not to go near any of these wild creatures." But Father smiled. "Rashida is happy," he said. "We can make her Australian kite sing."

Ama was holding the kite, looking at its torn paper. "This is what he could have done to you. He must have thought it was a live thing."

"But he didn't hurt us," said Rashida. "And he showed me where the kite was."

"He is a good Maharajah," said Lal.

Ama looked at him and then at all of us. "You will not go near him again," she said.

Outside, in the yard, Rashida said, "The High Maharajah of the Sky has given me my song, and I will thank him." She salaamed very solemnly towards the third hill and, after a moment when I almost laughed, so did Lal. And so did I.

THE SINGING MAN

WE were following the sound of bells when we heard the sound of singing. There was Rashida and there was me.

"Who's that?" I asked.

But she said nothing, just walked on as if she knew—the way she always did. And I followed her—the way I always did, the younger sister, the silly one, the question-asker. I followed her until we found the words:

O, the days of the Kerry dancing,
O, the clack of the wooden shoon...

I followed her until we found the singer, until he found us, the stranger, the new face, the shabby man who was sitting on our hill. He wanted to know what we were doing there.

"This is our place," said Rashida.

"We live here," I said. "We are looking for Yasmin."

"Would she be another of you?" He looked like an Australian—his face was red, like all the Australians—but his voice was different.

"She's one of our goats." I loved telling things; Rashida stood silent. "She runs away, and then she gets lost. She's only little and she gets frightened. We have to find her before dark comes. That's why we have the bells."

"Have you seen her?" said Rashida.

"Well, now." The man looked at her. "Could you be describing her?"

I was ready. "She's a dear little goat—"

"She's white." Rashida was sensible. "She wears a red collar."

"With silver bells and—"

"No-o." The man was doubtful. "No, I haven't been seeing her." He must have seen though that I would cry. "I wouldn't be worrying," he said. "Dark's nothing at all. And you know about goats when the night comes down. Don't you?" We were shaking our heads. "Don't you?" He was amazed at our ignorance. "They change into birds. Why, all the world knows it! And they're off and flying up in the trees. And they fluff out their feathers, safe from harm, warm as a parlour all night long. And when morning comes, they're all of them turning themselves back into goats again, into goats with bells on." He laughed then—at us, or at the goats with bells on, while I thought about the marvellous world of night-time when all the house was asleep. But Rashida was thinking about life.

"How do you know? Have you ever seen them?"

"I've read about it! In my books!" The stranger was indignant. "Plain as plain! Look!" He took a book from a big bag he had been leaning on and held out a page— printed!—for us to see.

"But we can't—"

Rashida grabbed my arm, to stop me talking, and she nodded her head as though she could read.

"We have to go home now." That was all she said.

We were at the bottom of the hill, still with the sound of ringing—but with a different song and with talk from ourselves—when we heard the tinkle of bells. So it was Yasmin, Rashida, and I who went home together to tell Father about the man on our hill who could sing and could read, and could tell him all about goats.

"But I know him," explained Father. "He is coming to do our books."

Uncle Seyed was against it. "This man," he said. "This man! Mr Johnson was a good man."

"Mr Johnson is away."

"I don't care," said Uncle Seyed. "You always talk nonsense. I am against it. This man, this man who knows all about goats is nothing but a stranger. He doesn't belong in our town. You don't even know his name. He's just the man who does the books—"

"I do know his name," said Father. He put his chuppatty down on the table, to leave his hands free. "He is Paddy-the-Drunk."

"Paddy-the-Drunk!" Uncle Seyed was furious; alcohol is forbidden to Muslims. Father laughed, and applauded him, but he explained very carefully to Ama our mother—and to us—that there was no need to worry. "He has worked all around here. He is sober at work, and kind, and is very good with the books. He is an educated man, from the city. They are bad times there. There are many with no work. I suppose that is why such an educated man has come to the country."

"If such an educated man who is Paddy-the-Drunk is working for us," said Ama, "why have you not brought him here to eat with us?"

Father looked all around the room, then he saw us. "He wants to be with the goats." He laughed, stopped suddenly, began to talk. "He has one of the huts down near the creek. He's going to cook for himself, clean for himself. He doesn't like women. He calls them nuisances, chattering nuisances. The other farmers say if a woman talks to him, is friendly, he packs up and goes—goes right away. We must leave him alone in the hut down by the creek."

"It is not right," said Uncle Seyed. "And I shall keep a watch on him."

We kept a watch on him, too, Rashida and I. He worked at the bench in the shearer's hut. The bench was covered with papers, and letters, and books and receipts on sharp-pointed files. We couldn't understand them, but we knew already that they never told stories, though Father and Paddy-the-Drunk seemed to think that they were important. Father used to call at the hut every morning on his way to the paddocks, and every morning he found us there before him, already away from breakfast and our kitchen work. He used to laugh at us, but he was serious when he gave Paddy his work for the day, more papers to add to those on the bench. Paddy worked at them all morning, leaning over the bench "as though it were an altar". But at lunch-time he talked to us. Ama let us spend lunch-time with him because she did not think it right that a man should eat alone.

And it was fun—for Rashida, Lal, our young brother, and me. He told us stories stranger than any we had heard—not about Krishna and tigers, not about blacks and kangaroos, not about anything we knew, but stories full of leprechauns and harps and Saint Patricks and mysterious beautiful pale women. Sometimes we did not understand his words, but the sound of them, the sing of them, was beautiful. Sometimes he used to take Lal, who was his favourite, on his knee and then he used to sing, when his sing-song words were finished, songs so beautiful—and so long—that we wanted to cry, Rashida and I. But Lal used to laugh and beg for more.

And Paddy taught us—it was one of the things he taught us—a song to sing, a song about someone who was "very like Lal" so Paddy said, called Patsy Fagan who was "a harum-scarum devil-may-careum laughing Irish boy". We used to wish that Paddy would stay forever. But our Paddy was only for the mornings, was only for lunch-time. In the afternoons, Paddy used to gather his own, his precious books and go off singing across the paddocks, away and beyond the second hill. He carried his books in his great book-bag and he would not let us go with him, even to carry the bag. He would tell us to watch him go, and we would stand there and watch and listen as his singing grew fainter and fainter until he was out of hearing. And sometimes we stood there even until he was out of sight. But Uncle Seyed was not like us.

One lunch-time Paddy said to us, "You know about Aladdin and his very famous lamp. Well, I have a genie all of my own—and I don't even own a lamp."

"What's a genie, Mr Paddy?" asked Lal.

"Ah, my boy, I hope you never know," said Paddy. It's a fearsome-looking black thing, it is. And it keeps appearing to me and at me, at my window, looking in. I was sitting at my bench, working away, innocent as a boy, at your father's papers and all, and I looked up and there it was—black as all hell, complete with turban."

"What did you do, Mr Paddy?"

"Why, I closed the window. But would you believe it, quicker than whisky it was round at the other side, peering and purring at the other window."

"What did you do then?" asked Rashida.

"I looked it square in the eyes." Paddy looked the way he did when he told us about Tyrone and the English Bastards. "Square in the eyes I looked it." He looked at us. And we looked at him. "Square in the eyes I looked it! And it disappeared like—magic!"

"Evil! Vile! White-man's stuff! I told you!" Uncle Seyed was enjoying dinner. "Do you know what he is keeping up in the hills, in second hill, your Paddy-the-Drunk? Bottles! Bottles of brandy!"

Ama and Father burst out laughing. "It is all very well to laugh," said Uncle Seyed. "It is a serious matter. Muslims do not have alcohol in their homes, on their properties."

"But he is never drunk here," Ama said. "He drinks in the hills because he respects our beliefs."

"How," said Father, "did you find out that he drinks in the hills?"

Uncle Seyed looked innocent. "I was just passing by and I saw him there. He was sitting on a rock and reading from some English book, drinking from a brown-coloured bottle. There were other bottles there among the rocks."

"But there's no reason why you should ever go to that hill."

"Oh, I just happened to pass there." Uncle Seyed looked more innocent. They laughed then, Father and Ama. "In any case," said Uncle Seyed, "there are only empty bottles there now. On my way back tonight I emptied all the bottles."

We told Paddy what Uncle Seyed had done. "Uncle Seyed thinks you are up to no good."

"Does he indeed?" said Paddy. He said nothing else, but he looked thoughtful. When we were going, he told us that he would not be going up the hill today. He thought he had better rest. He was not feeling well. But if we wanted to, we could play near the hut, though we must not make much noise.

"Are you very sick?" asked Lal.

"I don't know," said Paddy, in a whisper, "that you could call it sick. It's only my heart. The doctor told me—but I called him a fool—that I had to take brandy for to make it well. But there's no brandy now, not none in the world… " He shrugged his shoulders and went into the hut.

He may have spoken more loudly than he meant to because, just then, Uncle Seyed was passing.

Actually we saw a lot of Uncle Seyed that afternoon. He seemed always to be coming back to the house, always to be passing the window when Paddy's moanings and groanings were at their loudest. At last Uncle Seyed walked up to the door of the hut, opened it, and demanded to be told the truth.

"Are you sick?" he said.

Paddy cried out with pain, worse than before, horribly enough to make Lal cry.

"I will get the doctor," said Uncle Seyed.

"It's a kindness you're meaning," groaned Paddy, "and thank you for it. But you'd be doing no help at all getting me the doctor. It'd be better surely to be getting the priest. What could a doctor be giving me except brandy and its little warmth?" And he began to moan again.

Uncle Seyed went straight to his horse, got on it, and rode away.

"He's riding to town."

"Is he now?" Paddy sounded stronger, more like laughing. "I wouldn't be surprised now if that wicked genie wouldn't be buying a river of brandy to fill all the bottles that he emptied, and the man who was owning them, too."

We were still at the door of the hut talking to Paddy who was singing and laughing on his bed of pain, "Though it hurts me, my darlings, but I've got the gay heart". He was telling us about heaven and how its real name was Ireland and nursing Lal and calling him Seamus when Rashida called from the doorway that someone was coming. Paddy moaned and fell back on the bed. Lal began to fan him as he had been told to do. Rashida and I rushed to tuck him in. The four of us, conspirators, innocent and guilty together, listened to the footsteps as they came to the door.

"There are two people," said Rashida.

Paddy groaned.

"To carry the brandy, Mr Paddy?" said Lal.

"The doctor?" I said.

Paddy groaned louder than before.

They came through the doorway, Uncle Seyed and the priest. Paddy put his head under the blanket and gave a hollow, echoing, terrifying moan.

"Paddy McCarthy! Just what do you think you're doing?"

Quick as a sparrow, Paddy sprang upright in the bed.

"There's nothing wrong with your reflexes, Paddy McCarthy."

"No, it's the rest of me," said Paddy. "I'm dying, I am, and that black thing beside you, he could be telling you the reason why."

"I know the reason why. And it's a great shame you are to all men and the Irish to be moaning and groaning loud as ten healthy men like a great little baby and worrying people, lying like Sheba with a boy to fan you and hand-maidens to wait on you and Mr Seyed here to ride on his great wild horse and bring you more comfort than Solomon gave Sheba. Meaning me."

"It wasn't you I was wanting."

"But I'm the one who can tell you what you'll be getting." Father Harrigan stopped smiling and began now to speak in a voice like thunder of God and the devil, and of fires so terrible that all of us Muslims, even Uncle Seyed, felt at home. But not Paddy. He kept trying to interrupt, talking about jokes, hard work, his mother, anything that came into his head. It was no use. Father Harrigan went on to the end. Made Paddy a devil and Uncle Seyed a saint. "And now," he said, smiling at us children, "your lady mother has been promising me a curry of chicken. So we'll leave you, you hypocrite, to make yourself decent and then I will watch you at dinner."

"Oh, he doesn't eat with us. He doesn't like ladies."

"Paddy McCarthy, I'll not have you shaming the Irish like this. You'll get yourself up, and you'll get yourself shaved, and you'll eat with decent people, and you'll be a ladies' man for this one night or I'll see that you're nothing here or anywhere in the district."

So that night, that one night, Paddy (and Father Harrigan) ate with the family. And we were all glad, though Paddy sat sulking or shy while Father Harrigan played with the baby or talked with Ama, telling her stories about girls and weddings in Ireland and the beauties there that couldn't compare with her. He made us all laugh. And he laughed, too.

But Father was right: Paddy would not be sociable. He got up early and worked hard all the next day, and the next day, too. And then he was finished. His big book-bag hung round his hip, his sugar-bag of clothes hung on his shoulder, and he walked from the hut to the main gate. We followed him, the three of us, running, jumping, skipping, dancing.

"Where are you going? Why don't you stay? We love you, Mr Paddy. Why don't you stay? Mr Paddy? Mr Paddy . . . ?"

"I don't know," said Paddy. "I don't know why I'm going. I don't know where I'm going. But all my life I've been on the move. Walking agrees with me. It's all that I know—except my books."

"Don't you want a family? Don't you want friends? Don't you want a house with a fire and a kitchen?"

"But my books are my family, my books are my friends. And I tell you, my darlings, I'm going to a country where the sun's like a blessing and the rivers run rosy with a taste like—" He looked at us. "Taste like tea," he finished.

He laughed then and started down the road, beginning to sing. We were still calling out after him—"What country? Where? Goodbye!"—when he disappeared in the wattles at the turn of the road. Only his voice came back, growing fainter and farther:

> *"O, for one of those hours of gladness*
> *Gone, alas, like our youth too soon."*

THE CHILD THAT WINS

I WAS swinging on the gate and wondering if the day would ever end, if anything interesting would ever happen at all. Ama had called from the kitchen, called me to come and work, and the sound of her voice chased me the long way down the dusty track that led from the garden to the front gate of the property. And I swung on it, open and shut, shut and open, this way and that, sometimes on top—which made me frightened and pleased—and sometimes on the bottom rung, which pleased me, too, and was very safe. I was on top of the gate when I saw Hussein come through the trees and along the road towards me. I almost fell in my excitement. He was our like-a-cousin like-a-brother prince of story-tellers. He had been away to school. He had lived in the white men's cities, in houses where a hundred people lived in little cells like bees in a beehive. Or so he said. We were not sure it was true; it was in one of his stories. He had hundreds of them. He brought one with him every time he came to the house. A story and a present. The present was for us—the children. The story was for us, too, but everyone listened—Ama our mother, Father, Uncle Seyed. Uncle Seyed laughed and got angry and said they were lies, like white men's stories, but he listened all the same right to the end, as we all did, and asked for more. As we all did.

That was why they all came from the house when I ran back shouting that Hussein was coming. That was why no one scolded me for running from the garden and kitchen work. They just stood there on the veranda, waiting to greet him—the grown-ups—but we children ran at him, shouting our greetings and our jokes. When we got to him we salaamed formally before flinging ourselves on to him. He hugged Rashida and me and he threw Lal high into the air.

"Lal is a bag of wheat!" We screamed with laughter, but Hussein did not. He looked sad. He put Lal down.

"Lal is a nice boy," he said. "You're all nice children."

Rashida and I stopped laughing and looked at him with surprise. This was not the way he should have talked to us. He should have called us monkeys, mosquitoes, monsters, useless—anything but nice. Even Rashida and I knew that we were not nice. We were sure Hussein was sick or— terrible thought!— did not like us any more. Lal was not worried. He was six and a boy and already as vain as a man. He knew he was nice and just went on laughing.

On the veranda Hussein pushed us away. He bowed to Ama, Father, and to Uncle Seyed. He was greeting them politely, properly. This was strange, too.

"*Salaam Aleikum*," he said.

Ama must have been surprised. She took what seemed to be a long time before she answered. She must have been searching her mind for the Punjabi answer—"And peace be with you".

"*W'aleikum salaam*," she said at last. Then she broke into English, laughing. "But, Hussein, my son, why so polite, so thoughtless? That is not my language, is not yours. What has happened to our Australian boy who shakes hands with ladies and says 'how do you do'?"

"It doesn't matter how he talks. He's here. He'll tell us a story. Won't you, Hussein?" Lal caught hold of his hand, but Hussein did not lift him or fondle him or fight with him or do any of the things that he used to do. He handed him a bag of fruit.

"Mangoes from Bungabee," he said, "for the children." He should have thrown them at us, told us we were greedy, hoped they would keep us quiet, but now he meant us to take them like a present from a grown-up and go away. Even Lal was surprised. Hussein turned to Ama. "Begum," he called her, polite as anything. "I have had worries since I saw you last. I've had many things to think of. My mother sends you greetings, but that is not why I am here. She is worried about me and thinks that I should talk to you and

Muhummad Din." Uncle Seyed grunted and turned away. "And to Seyed our friend," Hussein added quickly.

Uncle Seyed nodded. "Your father," he said, "is he well?"

"It is not that," said Hussein. "He is very well—and very fierce."

Uncle Seyed snorted, we children looked interested. "A quarrel!" he said. "You young ones have no respect!" Uncle Seyed was always saying things like that and nobody minded, but suddenly Hussein was shouting at him, his voice trembling with anger.

"My father! My father," he was shouting, "is a stubborn, selfish bitter old man. He lives in he past. He thinks Australia's the Punjab. He does not understand me, just doesn't know the life I have. He won't listen, won't talk, won't try to understand—"

"My son, my son." Father was shocked and we children were fascinated. We had never dreamt—not ever—that anyone could speak of his parents like that, not any Muslim. We listened as our father answered him. "Your father is a good man. He has worked hard. All his life he has worked hard, to give his children the life they have, the things he never had."

"Lots of people have done that. You've done it," said Hussein. "But you're not like him. I can talk to you. You aren't always saying Punjabis do this, Punjabis do that, Muslims do so and so."

Uncle Seyed looked pleased. He had laid these very charges against our father. "Your father is a very good man," said Uncle Seyed.

"Your father was grown when he came to Australia," said Father. "His ways were already made. I was a boy. I lived here a long time, travelled a long way, saw many things—different people, different ways. I know this country better than I remember the Punjab. When you have two countries in your mind it is easy to fit them together."

"And my father has only one!" said Hussein. "Punjab! Punjab! Punjab!" He said the name over and over again and it sounded different from the way we had ever heard it before. It sounded like a quali song, endless and boring, close to tears.

"But what's wrong?" said Ama. "Sit down and tell me. Tell me straight away."

"I am going to be married," said Hussein. The grown-ups looked astonished, and we children were surprised. "I think," said Hussein.

"Married," said Ama.

"It's not so strange," said Hussein. "I am twenty-two."

"Twenty-two," said Father. "I had forgotten."

"You children grow so quickly," said Ama.

"Marry who?" said Uncle Seyed. "No one to marry! You have to go to Bungabee, Fiji, to the Punjab."

"Who do you want to marry?" said Ama.

"Have you chosen?" said Father.

"Ah!" Uncle Seyed took one look at Hussein's miserable face. "This is the quarrel," he announced.

"I'm going to marry the teacher," said Hussein. "I think."

There was silence—children, stories, mangoes, manners, everything was forgotten. No one remembered to send us out of hearing. No one had anything to say. Even Uncle Seyed looked thunderstruck. Hussein was the only one who had any words at all, and they poured out of him like rice from a bursting bag.

"And my father," said Hussein. "My father does not approve. Calls her a Christian, an eater of pig. He says she is white and I am black, our children will be yellow and brown and not belong anywhere. Her people will despise us and we will have no place. He says her ways are not our ways, that I am a traitor to Allah and to India. He wants me to marry some simpering silly who will cry when I am angry, who'll cook me nothing but rice and know nothing that I know. He has written to Fiji. He has found someone I don't know, who doesn't know me, doesn't even speak English. What would I do with her? With such a wife? Anne is a good girl. I have known her a long time—since I started accountancy. You remember how kind she was. I told you about her— how she came in the shop while I was working at lessons, how she helped me with English, words none of us knew. She has helped me always. I am clever with figures, but I would not have passed if she had not helped me. Everyone knows that—even my father. He asked her to dinner and now he talks like this. He thanked her himself and now he calls her a pig. Her people can bear me, but he will not bear her. I have met her parents, and we were like friends. But my father now will not talk to her even. You think that I am angry, but I'm only ashamed to have such a parent and belong to such people."

"But she is Christian," said Uncle Seyed. And that was that.

Ami looked at him sadly. "It is a difference," she said. "Differences are very hard, and married is a long time."

"But she is not different," said Hussein. "She is like me. And we can talk. I tell her things—stories, dreams, hopes, things I could not tell anyone else. And I want to marry her. She wants to marry me. She doesn't think about difference. She is like me."

"Unbelievers! You, her, two of you!" Uncle Seyed was furious. "Your father is right!"

"Hussein," said Father, "you were a little boy when your father first sent you to me for advice about school. I was proud of his trust and proud I could help, because although I am a man from the villages, I know about Australia. And after that, when you came here because you wanted to, I was more proud and more. And always, somehow, because I loved you and knew you, I found the words to tell you things, to help. Now you have grown away from me, passed me. I cannot find words."

"Then you despise me," said Hussein. "You."

"No, no," said Father while Uncle Seyed muttered. "You are a man now. I had not thought of that. And neither had your father. It is time now for you to find the words yourself. I remember the old country and I know the new one. But the country you live in is strange to me, and to your father. You were born here, and your ways are no ways that we can know."

"And if he loses the way?" Ama sounded worried and annoyed and gentle, the way she scolded Lal when he did not behave like a good Punjabi boy. "If he chooses wrong? What then? If his father is right and a boy like Hussein belongs nowhere except with people who remember the old ways?"

"I don't know, I don't know." Father stroked Lal's head in a tired way. He looked very old. "Hussein will find that out, and he must stay with it and bear it until the end, until the wrong thing is the right thing or until it doesn't matter any longer what is right or what is wrong."

Uncle Seyed was mumbling bitterly in Punjabi that that time could never be, that what was right was right for ever, and that what was Muslim was always right. No one answered him, but Hussein stood up.

"There is nothing to say. My father has said all of the words, and I have tried to answer. He says I must give up all thought of this marriage or I must leave his house, must never come there. Well, I will never come there."

"You must come to us often." Father put his arm round Hussein's shoulder. "You are our son, too."

Ama went to him and put her hands together in Hindu blessing and farewell. She bent her head. "I, too, left my father's house. I, too, married someone from a different world, a different faith. I have known pain, and I have known joy. It will be like that for you. All ways become the right way."

Next morning he arrived — Shareef Khan, the huge, the terrible, the shopkeeper, the prayer-leader, Hussein's father. He stood on the veranda, where Hussein had stood, in his navy-blue suit with the stripe in it, in his waistcoat with its gold watch-chain. He played with the chain as he talked and we longed to play with it, too, but all he offered us was the umbrella that he carried on every hot day and we had to put that away.

"Ah! Children! Children!" said Shareef Khan, mopping his head with the sheet that he used as a handkerchief. "If only they stayed like yours! If only they would not grow!" He did not wait for any comment. "My dear friend, you understand. It is not that the girl is not respectable. But what of their children? They will belong nowhere."

"They will belong to both worlds," said Ama.

"Yes, yes," said Shareef Khan. "That is true out here on the farm, but what do you know of the town and the city and the time to come?"

"People are people," said Ama.

"Your own is your own," said Uncle Seyed.

"If you stay anywhere long enough," said Father, "people get used to you. They take you in to their houses and their ways."

"Muhummad Din," said Shareef Khan, his fat round face as earnest as Ramadan, "Were we wrong to come here? Were we wrong to have children in a country not their own, living with people not their own, seeing ways that are not theirs?"

"I have wondered," said Father, "but I do not know the answer or if there is any answer. One thing, only, I know. Our children are not us. Our ways are not theirs. And our people, the people we remember, are no longer theirs. They will marry as they please. There is nothing we can do. We do not know what is for the best."

"I know," said Uncle Seyed.

"We could have stayed in India." Shareef had prepared his speech and was not to be diverted. "We could have stayed in clay huts in the Punjab and have watched our children hungry, untaught, poor — as we were. But we wanted better for them. Better! Is this better? I am afraid. I am afraid for my son's sons. They will be educated, they will be well, but where will they belong? I am afraid for my wife and even for me. This girl — her parents — they are educated, they are Christians, what can they have in common with us?"

"They are nice people," said Father. "Hussein has met them and he says—"

"Hussein is a child."

"Hussein is a man," said Father.

"But it is best," said Shareef Khan, "That we never see him again. And we will not. And even his name—I will not hear it again."

Allah rights everything in His good time. They had been married a long time, Hussein and his Anne, and they had a child, a son who laughed. Of course we knew. Hussein and Anne had brought him to show us and Ama had cooked saffron rice with almonds and raisins and kababs with steak and coconut and pineapple and tamarind sauce and a thousand things for a first-born's feast. But Shareef Khan was not there, and he did not know. Ama told his wife, and although she came for five minutes to see the baby, her first grandchild, she dared not mention it to Shareef Khan. At the mention of the name "Hussein" he would go red as a pomegranate, crying on God and all wise things to acknowledge that justice was dead and the young like serpents bit at their parents.

Hussein and Anne lived in the town in tiny rooms. Hussein was determined to save enough to open his own office— Hussein Khan, Accountant. He was working for the bank, and working for himself, doing books for farms, for anyone who would pay him.

One night he came home, from twelve miles out, as tired as tired. As he climbed the stairs towards his room with a kitchen he suddenly heard the great booming voice of Shareef Khan. He was so surprised that he stopped on the stair and heard his son scream and his wife's soft voice. The gladness he felt gave way to anger—the father that denied him was bullying them all, waking his son and booming at his wife. He ran up the stairs, flung open the door, ready to rage. He stood there amazed. Anne was smiling. His father was laughing and roaring endearments at the astonished child he held in his arms. With his free hand he was swinging his watch-chain just beyond the baby's reach.

"Aha!" said Shareef Khan. "He is here, the good-for-nothing. He has come home at last, the scoundrel that I called my son. Salaam, salaam, O Great High Lord who descended to earth to marry, it is good of you to crawl home to your wife and child you abandoned in this terrible small room, even though it is the middle of the night. Shabash! Good on you!" Shareef was laughing at his own Australian-ness and roaring in his half-pretended anger. "Anne, Anne," he said, "is this how he keeps you? A room like a coolie's hut and a son that he does not see except in the night when good sons are sleeping! Why was I not told that this son had been born? This is my grandchild, the son of sons, and this Hussein, this walker in dirt, tells me no word of it. If you had not a good wife, I would never have known! Come here, you nothing, come here."

Meek as a lamb, like an obedient son, Hussein went to him.

"Here! Here!" yelled Shareef. "Don't stand there like a lump of lead, you fool! Take these gold bangles and put them on your son as every decent father does."

Hussein just stood there, like a lump of lead, looking at the bangles with their inscriptions from the Koran.

"Take them! Take them! Use them!" His father was ordering him, or pleading with him. No one knows which.

"Yes, father," said Hussein meekly, and he took the bangles.

Shareef watched him put them on the boy's arms, watched the boy bite at them.

"You see," he said to Anne, "the child always wins in the end."

THE DRAGON
OF KASHMIR

IT was the heat of summer, the holiday time, and all of us— Ama, Father, we children—had come away from the farm and its bare, glazed hills. We had come to the North Coast country, the world near Nambucca. The grass was green and gentle and the blue of Krishna was everywhere—in the sky, in the sea, in the puddles after rain, in every drop of water that you held to look at. We stayed with the Shahs.

They were nice people. Everyone liked them, but not really me. The children were brave, when I was shy. They were quick, when I was slow. They were Australian, and not like me. They had always had white friends, when I had had only Rashida. Rashida liked them. Sometimes it frightened her— the games they played, the way they talked— but she could do the same. She was braver than I, she was older. It was Grandmother Shah that I liked.

She was old and gentle. And I think that she was sad. She had come to Australia from Kashmir. She had come a long time ago, when she was young and Grandfather Shah was young, too. And now he was dead and her children were grown, and her grandchildren were brittle with Australian ways and Australian talk and had no time to listen to her. There was no one alive who remembered her. She was Grandmother Shah—even to Ama, my mother, who had also come from Kashmir.

But I listened to her. I asked her questions and pestered her to tell of the old days and the old ways, to tell me stories of Grandfather Shah and the days when he trained camel-drivers for the long rides through Australia, stories of Kashmir and the jewels that the Indian Maharanis wore. She scolded me and called me a Bengali, said that I chattered like monkeys, that I was wearing her out, that I should play with the other children and I should be quiet—the way Kashmiri children were quiet—and should never ask questions. But, always, she answered me. Only, sometimes, her answers were so long and so slow, so full of memories that she seemed to forget that I was there. She would look at me and not see me, so that I had to chatter again and to prod her with words to bring her back to the story. I had to call her "Grandmother" to make her look at me.

She was not my grandmother. She was not related to my family at all, except by friendliness.

It was for friendliness, or to keep me quiet, that she let me look through the old cardboard boxes that held her memories —ribbons and letters, photographs and brooches. We were in the garden. Grandmother Shah sat in her chair in the shade of the tamarind-tree and crocheted. I sat on the grass near her and went through one of the boxes.

It was a warm day, but nice and lazy, and I pulled the old things out tiredly and looked at them as though looking were a very hard job. I was watching how slowly my hand moved when I was lifting them—the envelopes with their faded stamps and the letters covered with writing in Hindi. It was then, under a heap of letters, that I found the fan.

It was old. Some of the sticks were broken. But it was silk, and big. It was bright, but faded. I opened it and fanned myself like an Indian lady or a Maharani. But it was full of dust that made me sneeze. So, sneezing, and laughing, and chattering like a monkey, I jumped up and dropped it on Grandmother Shah's lap, on her crochet work. She did scold me then. I had made her white work dirty. I was stupid and thoughtless. I was Australian and not well bred. And what was I doing with a filthy old fan?

"But, Grandmother, it's yours. It was in your box. Wasn't it yours? Who did it belong to? Did she have a story? Can you remember?"

Grandmother Shah had brushed the fan to the ground, but now she picked it up and looked at it. She looked for a long time. I was bored.

"Grandmother Shah!"

"Bring me that box. It was in that box?"

She looked through the things in the box, and then pulled out an envelope that had a photograph inside it. It was very old and faded, but she held it and looked at it as if it were new. I leant on the arm of her chair and looked at it, too. It was very old and faded. It was not new at all.

It showed two girls in a garden. They stood very close to one another and the hems of their saris were touching. They both had long black plaited hair and caste-marks on their foreheads. One of them held the fan—but it was a new fan then.

"There's something on it," I said. I opened it—the real fan—and looked hard at the faded silk. "It's a dragon."

"The dragon of Kashmir," said Grandmother. "I remember it now." She took the open fan from me, and held it. "It was bright green then, and the dragon was silver. It was not the kind of fan that a young girl should have."

"Did you know them, Grandmother — the girls in the picture?"

"That one is me," she said. "That was when I was Farida, and not Grandmother. That was when I was fourteen, and not here. That was in Kashmir." She laughed, at the picture. "They are Kashmiri roses," she said.

"They're withered and brown."

"It is the photograph that has withered," said Grandmother Shah. "That was the garden of our house in Kashmir, my father's house. I remember it all now—the day the photograph was taken. It was my brother. He had come back from Oxford, from the big school there. He had come back the night before. He was wearing English clothes. He forgot to take off his shoes at the door. He was like a stranger, but he was still ours. And in the morning he said, 'I will photograph you all.' But we didn't know what that meant and we thought that photographed might be like—baptized, or vaccinated, or something nasty. And then he came out of the house with the box on legs and he made us all stand still and look at it. He said that we would see a bright yellow bird. But we did not. None of us did."

"The other girl is holding the fan." I knew all about photographs.

"It is hers," said Grandmother Shah. "We were both fourteen—Lala and I."

"You're smiling," I said. "You're smiling in the photograph, and now, too."

"We were both fourteen. We thought that wonderful things would happen."

"And didn't they? You came to Australia."

"I came to Australia," said Grandmother Shah. "But I never wanted to go away. I wanted to be home. I wanted to be married, with children, a house with servants and the people that I knew. Lala is the one that should have come away. She wanted never to stay at home. She used to say— I remember how she used to tell me about countries a long way off where women walked like men. I used to say to her, 'The woman is the sole of the husband's foot.' It made her angry. Every time, it made her angry. I said it to her that morning. 'My brother is home,' I said. 'He is very fierce and white and handsome. He will make you want to be the sole of his foot.' "

"Did he?"

"No. Yes. She was very shy with him. Perhaps she loved him. She was shyer every day. Every day we saw him. She was my great friend, but she was the one who talked. She was very grown up. She used to talk no matter who was in the room—even if there were real adults there, even if there were men. But when my brother came into the room, she was quiet. All that summer she carried this fan. It was not the kind of fan that a young girl should have had, but it had been her mother's before it was hers. I remember now, when he was there, how slowly she used it; how she held it almost to hide her face. And the next year I came to Australia to be married, and Lala came with her father to the ship."

"Did she give you the fan then? As a present?"

"I cannot remember. I remember how I cried and how she told me that I was only a child, that I should be proud to be free and going away—even if it did mean that I had to be married and become nothing."

"Was your brother there?"

"He was there. With his wife."

"Was Lala his wife?"

"Oh, Nimmi, child! Nothing wonderful ever happens, ever."

"Did she get married?"

"Who should she marry? She was more clever than any man in Kashmir. Her father used to let her help him. She would never have been Grandmother, and not Lala."

"Is she dead then?"

Grandmother looked at the photograph. "We were fourteen then," she said. "We are both dead now. I am Grandmother Shah and no one remembers Farida. She is as old as I am and she has never left Kashmir."

"But I remember you!"

"You remember what I tell you, and that is all you will remember."

I waved the fan, slowly, almost hiding my face. I peeped at Grandmother Shah. "Do I look like Lala?" I said.

But grandmother was looking at the photograph with its brown faded flowers in Kashmir, and its brown faded faces.

"Why do they have dragons on Kashmiri things?" I was peering at the design on the fan.

"Because they eat everything. Because they live for ever." She put the photograph down on the ground and picked up her crochet work.

"If she didn't give you the fan, then you ought to send it back."

"Stop chattering, child."

The wind picked at the photograph. I moved to grab it.

"Let it go," said Grandmother. Almost, she shouted. "Let it go!"

And the two of us sat there—as though it were that time again—and watched the wind lift the photograph and then drop it, tug it and push at it, lift it and lever it till suddenly it went up high, high, and whirled round in the sky that was as blue as Krishna.

"It will blow away," I said. "You will never see it again."

"The dragon will eat it," said Grandmother Shah. She went back to her crochet work.

THE BABU
FROM BENGAL

SHE was sitting in the sun and I called out to her.

"Grandmother Shah!"

"Ah, Nimmi," she said. She opened her eyes. "It is you, is it, come to destroy my peace again?"

"They sent me," I said. They sent me. I have to tell you that a stranger has come to the house. He is called the Babu from Bengal."

"That is not his name, not his title, child. That is what he is."

"What is he?"

"He is a babu, a Hindu who can read and write, a clerk, a half-educated educated man."

"I can read and write. What good is half-educated? Am I a babu, too?"

"Babus are Hindus like me. You are a Muslim. And you are not even half educated yet. You have very bad manners."

"What do babus do?"

"Questions and questions! They write letters for people who are not educated at all."

"Is the Babu going to write a letter for you?"

"No, no, no!" Grandmother Shah was laughing. "He has not written a letter for anyone since The Quarrel."

"What quarrel?"

"Stories and stories! It was a long time ago. It was then, and this is now . . . "

Then there were lots of our people here—Punjabis like your father's people, Pathans like my husband's. They were all Muslims. Only the Babu and I were Hindus.

I remember the first time I saw him. My husband was away with the camel teams. I was staying on his brother's farm. It was a lonely time for me. My brother-in-law had his farm to busy him. His wife had her children. At that time, I had none of my own. They were good to me, they welcomed my visits, but their ways were not my ways and they did not remember me or anything that I had ever known. Only my husband could remember. I was glad to see a Hindu come to the farm.

He drove up to the house in his wagon. We heard him before we could see him. It was an old wagon and it made a clicking, rattling noise like pieces of wood being hit together. It was wood. And when we went out to look at it, we saw a great sign saying "HURRI CHANDA MUKERJI, CLERK B.A."— and written beside the B.A. in very small letters, the one word, "*failed*".

The Babu looked then the way he looks now. He had steel-rimmed glasses and wore white clothes. He had bandy legs and he had no teeth. He wore an enormous turban and he seemed to be bowing to you all the time. It may have been good manners, but I think, I really think, it was the weight of his turban. He had come to write up the farmers' books, to write what letters they needed. His fees were high, but he was known and necessary. I remember how politely he stood in front of my brother-in-law, listening and hardly speaking, his head nodding with agreement or the weight of his turban.

But with me he was different. To me he could talk. And how we talked that first time! The places he had seen in his travels in India, the places that were home to me, the last time he had celebrated diwali, how his young brothers had flung red powder into his face to celebrate the birth of spring, how his mother had hung a sacred thread round his neck the day he was to leave the village. How she cried and said that she would never see him again! And these were things that any Hindu knew. "I remember," I kept saying, "I can remember… " and I cried, too. "I will never see any of it again."

"You will, you will," said the Babu. "When you are rich, and all the camels carry gold, you will go home. I will go home. My mother will see me again. I will give her back the sacred thread."

He never went, and neither did I. We did not realize then that Australia was home.

When the walk was ended, the reminding and remembering finished, there were other things to remember. There was now. The Babu was not happy. "Money," he moaned. "Money. Where is it? Who has it? How can a poor man get it? These Muslims—these Muslims!—they will not write letters. They know nothing of love. They write letters of business, letters to governments, letters of money—they ask me to write them two letters a year."

It was because of this that he started The Quarrel.

He was doing the books at Ishak Khan's place. Ishak was boasting, as his son does now, about the wonder of his farm, the lushness of the grass, the sleekness of the cows, the Muslim magnificence of his tomatoes. "Is it true then," said the Babu with gentle surprise, "your farm is doing well?"

"Of course my farm is doing well!"

"I was wrongly informed then," said the Babu. "Or perhaps I misunderstood."

"Who? Who?" growled Ishak Khan. "Who has wrongly informed you?"

"I was talking the other day to your neighbour Mahmoud Ali—"

"Mahmoud Ali! What did the liar say?"

"He only said that he had heard that your cows had the disease. He warned me against eating your beef—"

"My beef is perfect! It is killed the proper way! I will force this Mahmoud Ali to eat it. He will see if my cattle is sick!"

He should, of course, have forced the meat upon the Babu. He should, of course, have remembered that no Hindu would eat beef anyway. But "should" is a difficult word, and Ishak Khan was an angry man; "should" is a humble word, and Ishak Khan was a proud man. He roared with anger, roared like cattle. His wife and sons came running.

"Wretch!" he was shouting. "Wretch! Evil, jealous wretch!" He was moving towards the door, his great fists clenched, his great voice muttering insults. It was as if he were going straight to Mahmoud Ali's farm. He was stopped by the Babu's gentle Hindu voice.

"Mahmoud Ali deserves your anger," he was saying, "but I do not think it is wise to go up to his house."

"Wise? Wise? What is wise to do with a wretch who pretends to be a friend?"

"Wise is to do with everything," said the Babu. "If you go to the house Mahmoud Ali will call out a greeting. He will wish you peace. He will call you brother. He will welcome you formally into his house. It is, I believe, the custom among the Muslims. You will not be able to insult him then, it would be impolite."

Ishak Khan nodded. "True," he said.

"True," said his wife and sons. And they nodded, too.

"If I may be permitted to offer a suggestion." The Babu was soft and gentle, like a snake. "A letter," he suggested.

"Yes! A letter! A letter to make him ashamed! A letter!" They were all in agreement—Ishak Khan, his wife, his sons, the Babu. "I will sit down and write it now," said Ishak Khan.

"No. No. No," said the Babu. "If you write in your language, you must preserve the forms. You must begin with greetings, with blessings on his house and family. You should write in English. That is the language for business and rudeness. If you wrote in English, he could not mistake your feelings."

"True. True," said Ishak Khan. He nodded as he thought about it. His wife and his sons, they nodded, too. So did the Babu.

"You will write this letter for me now," he said to the Babu. "I cannot write English. The letter will start Dear Bad Friend . . .

The Babu kindly wrote the letter, and kindly collected his fee. He delivered it to Mahmoud Ali's, and collected the fee for delivery. The letter was beautifully phrased so as to have effect and to give no reason for its tone and anger. It was a savage, unprovoked attack and, after a suggestion from the Babu, Mahmoud Ali dictated a reply. The Babu collected his fee.

Letter followed letter—letters written down by the Babu, letters for which the Babu was paid, letters the Babu delivered. The insults grew bigger and the letters grew longer. The Babu's fees became greater. His pockets were as heavy as his turban. At Ishak Khan's, at Mahmoud Ali's, he bowed and nodded, whether from weight of turban or heaviness of pockets or the need to be polite, no one will ever know. All that the rest of us knew was that the quarrel was fierce and forever, that neither farm would hear a good word of the other, and that the Babu buzzed between the two of them like a blowfly.

The men talked of it—The Quarrel. "There has been nothing like it," said Ben Yussouf, "since little Zaffir Din stole the Chinaman's bike."

"It is that Bengali bandit," said Shak Ali. "All Bengalis are bad, but the Babu is the worst of them all."

"I will grab that Hindu," said Big Cassim, "by his skinny unwashed neck. And I will throw him out of the district." He flexed his muscles and blew out the ends of his moustache as though he were the fiercest of the warriors of Afghanistan. The others laughed at him and cheered him and shouted as though he were a wrestler. "Shabash! Hurrah! Shabash!"

"Children," said old Ben Yussouf. "You are like children. The Hindu is more clever than you. We know that he cheats us. He knows that we know. We know that he is trouble, but what are we without him? If we send him away, who will do the books, who will write to the Government?"

"My son will," said Wali Husson. They stared at him. "I sent him to Lismore. It was not to work in my brother's shop. It was not for reasons that I told you. It was so that he could go to school."

"School!"

"Yes, school," said Wali Husson. "It is a year since I paid a penny to the Babu. My son can write my books, and write my letters. His teachers are proud of him, and so am I." Nobody spoke and Wali Husson went on, getting more and more excited. "It is time that what we are thinking should be words. We are farmers. Our fathers were farmers. Our fathers' fathers were farmers. That was the way in the old country. But old days have old ways. It is different now. Our children were born here, this is all they know. Here you can choose. They may not want to be farmers. They may not want to marry farmers. We did not want to leave India, but we came here. We wanted for our children more than hunger and work. And what do we do, what are you all doing? The white people send their children to school. We send ours to work in the paddocks. The white children are learning to choose. Ours are learning to be farmers, peasants, people the Babu can use to make money from. This is because their fathers are stubborn and dislike change."

They were all silent, disturbed, looking at him and his excitement and pride. They had forgotten The Quarrel. They were thinking of the Babu and their need for him, of Mahmoud Ali's five daughters who must marry or be nothing because they had not been taught to choose, of their own children who were learning nothing but the work of the farm.

"It is the women," said Ben Yussouf. "The mothers would cry."

"The mothers would cry," said Sha Ali. "They want their own things near them. It is harder for them. We have our farms. We understand this country. We work with the earth. We know it and it's ours. We have white men as friends. But our women have no such owning, no such friends. This is not their country and its ways are not their ways. They live only in their homes, only with their children."

"They are afraid," said Ben Yussouf. "They do not want their children to despise them, to take the white men's ways and to think their mothers ignorant."

"I sent my son away," said Wali Husson. "I sent away the child of my heart. His mother prayed, begged, cried. Oh, how she cried! But I went out into the fields and worked my land. I did not let her see me cry. And soon, like me, she found that there was no time for tears—there were the cows to milk, the chickens to feed, the chuppatties to make. And now my son loves her really; he misses her."

"Sense!" said Shak Ali. "These are words of sense. I will send my children to school." The other men agreed to do the same.

"And now," said Ben Yussouf, "now that we have Wali Husson's son to help us, we will go to the Babu."

They went to him in a body and told him politely—because Ben Yussouf insisted they were not to demean themselves in front of a Hindu—that his services were no longer required, that it would be more convenient if he left immediately.

The Babu was not surprised. He was used to being found out. There was nothing to be done. Like a good Hindu, he accepted the facts and packed his wagon. And then, like a bad Hindu, drove off shouting insults as he went.

Everyone expected that Ishak Khan and Mahmoud Ali would now become friends. But everyone was wrong. Pathans are stubborn, and proud, and unforgiving. Explanation was useless, cursing the Babu was useless, neither of the "friends" would make the first move, although, of an evening, Mahmoud Ali would look out towards Ishak Khan's farm and say, "There is a lucky man." But it was not the farm he was thinking of; it was Ishak Khan's children. Ishak Khan had sons, and Mahmoud Ali had none. He had his five daughters and he loved them. But what were they except dowries to pay, weddings to arrange, trouble and expenses? "Ishak Khan is a happy man," he explained to Ben Yussouf. "It is sad that he has such a mean nature."

The men of the district had another meeting. They boasted of what their children were doing in the white people's school and then, only then, did they talk about The Quarrel—which was the reason they had met. "In my eighty years," said Ben Yussouf, "there has never been such foolishness."

They were all talking, suggesting ways to make the two "friends" friends when, suddenly, they heard a great shouting, a roaring like a bull. It was Ishak Khan.

"Quick! Quick!" he said. "We have to go over to Mahmoud Ali's. Mahmoud Ali has had a son! One of the girls came over to tell my wife. He's had a son! That forgotten son of Allah has been given a son." Ishak Khan was dancing with excitement, while the others stared at him. But when he made them understand, it was he who led them to Mahmoud Ali's.

Mahmoud Ali was standing at the door, proud as the day, for no man is a man until his son of sons is born. But when Ishak Khan grabbed him by the arm and cheered him, and laughed at him, and mocked him, and praised him, he could do nothing but cry—with joy for the son, and with joy for the friend.

What a celebration there was at Mahmoud Ali's that night! The girls had been cooking all day and the women had come over to help them in the afternoon. But no one had expected a son—this was the joy of joys. How everyone laughed! How they joked as they put money in the plate for the new boy! And when it was all over—the eating, the joking, the singing, the praising—then it was quite late. The hurricane lamps cast big shadows on the walls. The young children slept against their parents. The bigger ones whispered of school and the grown-ups talked of the old days and the old ways, remembered the world that used to be theirs.

"I remember," said Grandmother Shah. "I remember then as if it were now."

"But the Babu?"

"But the Babu?"

"Oh, he was clever!" Grandmother Shah was laughing. "Who could be angry at a time like that? While they all sat talking, there was a gentle knocking at the door. When Mahmoud Ali opened it, there stood the Babu, bobbing like a cork in water under the weight of his enormous turban and softly—oh, so softly—offering felicitations. He had bought a store in the town, and he wanted our custom. And, of course, in a way he was our friend; we were used to him. So we welcomed him and he sat down next to me and talked to me about the Hindu world that used to be ours."

"Where are you going? Tell me some more."

"But the Babu is up at the house. I must go and talk with my friend."

GRANDFATHER TIGER

GRANDFATHER Tiger was a secret and he lived at the bottom of the garden. He was Joti's tiger and no one else in the world dreamt of him. She had found him there by the river after Grandfather died. Wonderful Grandfather that you could talk to had died and left Joti with no one to tell how she missed him—only the tiger. She had found him when she was crying by the river. She had looked up and there he was, terrible and beautiful, like the gold-silk tiger on the cushion in the room that used to be Grandfather's.

And the tiger's voice was growly and kind, the voice of Grandfather. And Joti told him everything.

So this day she ran down the yard that, until this day, had been almost her only world. She ran as fast as she could, her bare feet hardly touching the ground, to tell Grandfather Tiger her great news. He was there—the way he always was now—behind the clump of lantana, on a grassy bank, at the river's edge.

She made the Hindu sign of greeting, joining her hands gently before her face.

"Salaam, Tiger Sahib," she said. "I am going to school."

"Salaam," said the tiger. "You have everything to learn."

"And I will wear a dress, like the other girls. I will be the same."

The tiger swished his tail and smiled, very tired. "A dress cannot make you the same," he said. "It will only be pretending."

Joti looked at him, scared. Grandfather had once said something like that.

"Will school not be good?" she asked in a little voice.

"Perhaps," said the tiger. "Perhaps there will be friends there."

"Friends!" said Joti. "Friends!" She smiled, danced two steps, salaamed, and hurried back to the house where her mother was calling her to dinner.

Their home was in the suburbs and Joti's father, Raj, went every day into the city to his work, like any father in the suburbs. Her mother stayed home with the children, and sometimes took Joti with her up to the shops, like any mother in the suburbs. And their house was like all the houses in their bushy suburb.

The house was the same, but the home was different, because Joti's parents kept the customs of their people. They took off their shoes before entering the house. They decorated the garden path for the Hindu Festivals. They cooked curry and rice and chupatties. The friends who came there for dinner sat on the floor and felt at home.

Dinner was always a formal affair and the children never sat down to it with the grown-ups. Joti, who was the eldest, stood near the table and passed whatever was required. She had to be quick enough to do this before she was asked, and polite enough never to seem in the way. But this night she made mistakes. She could think of nothing but school.

"The little one is going to school tomorrow," said Raj, her father, to excuse her. "She can think of nothing else."

Old Ram-Sukal, the guest of the evening, smiled at Joti. "You are going to become a clever lady, like your mother," he said.

Everyone laughed but Grandmother.

"Oh, it is not right for her to go!" she said. "It is not right! She will learn the white people's ways and think we are ignorant. She will call me stupid."

"No, Mother, no," said Raj. "My children must learn to live here. They cannot stay in the house always. They must learn all they can. Then they can go to India and teach what they know."

"They have never known India," said Ram-Sukal. "They may not wish to go."

"But now that India is free," said Raj, "there is so much to be done. Schools to be built, and hospitals, and people will be needed to run them. India will be great again."

"I thought," said Ram-Sukal, "that you were an Australian."

"I am. I was born here," said Raj. "But my people—"

"Your people," said Ram-Sukal. "I have been back and I have seen your people. There is a line through your father's village. Who are your people? Are you Indian or Pakistani? They will kill you if you do not know."

"Old friend," said Raj, shamefaced, "old friend, you are always right and always wise. But what are we to do? I belong here. I am Australian, but who will believe me? My skin, my face, my thinking contradicts me, and who will accept me—or my children?" He looked at Joti.

"Accept you!" said Grandmother. "You talk like a child. It is you that must accept. Can't you understand?" She looked round at them all. Do not let us part, she thought. Do not let us part.

Next morning was first-day-at-school morning, and Joti put on her white girl's dress. She fixed it in front of the mirror and hurried downstairs to show it and to get Grandmother to plait her hair. The family looked at her doubtfully.

Her arms and legs are so thin, thought her mother.

She looks ridiculous, thought Grandmother.

"I look beautiful," said Joti, and she smiled.

She went to school alone because she insisted, and Miss Adams, the teacher, was there on the veranda looking out for her.

"Hullo, Josie," she said. She had thought about this new girl, off and on, ever since she had interviewed her mother. She was a difficult case and her enrolment card was going to be a worry. The cards had a space to tick for 'Australian' and another space to tick for 'New Australian'. What was to be done with a dark-faced Indian child who was a second-generation Australian?

"Come in, dear," said Miss Adams. "You had better sit there." She pointed to an empty desk.

Joti sat in it, on the side nearest the window. Suddenly she felt a sharp poke in the back.

"That's where Dorothy sits," said a red-headed girl from the desk behind her. "You have to sit on the other side."

Joti wriggled across. "I'm sorry, I am sorry," she said. But the two girls behind didn't hear her. They went on whispering between themselves. And all day, whenever Miss Adams spoke to Joti, she called her Josie.

At playtime no one spoke to Joti, though they kept looking at her and giggling.

At lunch-time they were bolder. One of them spoke to Joti and the others laughed.

"You're awfully skinny," she said.

Joti smiled at her. She didn't know what to say. She didn't think it right to tell the girl that she was awfully fat.

They all watched her as she unwrapped her lunch. They all stared as she began to eat.

"What are you eating?" said one of them.

"Only kababs," said Joti.

"Kababs!" The girls sniggered at the word.

"That's only what black people eat," said the red-headed girl. "And I know what they're made of." She whispered something and the girls that heard her opened wide their eyes.

"Eating *those*!" said one girl. They all gazed at Joti.

She sat there as long as she could and, then, she gathered up her lunch and walked to the far end of the playground. She sat there, with her back to them so that they could not see her crying.

She started home from school very slowly, thinking of the endless number of days that school would be. Then she began to run, run as if bears were chasing her. She did not stop running until she had reached her home, raced through the front gate and was standing in the yard.

Everything was the same. The babies were playing on the lawn. There was the smell of curry cooking. It was her own home, safe and the same. She took off her shoes at the door and went quietly in.

As soon as she was in her room, Joti took off her new dress and put on her old sulwa. Then she went down the yard to talk to the tiger.

He was lying in his favourite spot by the river, and he stretched content-edly as Joti greeted him.

"It was horrible, horrible!" said Joti. "There are no friends there. They think I am black-people. They laugh at me, and I hate them."

"Ha!" said the tiger. "I thought that might happen."

"Then what am I to do?" said Joti. "What am I to do?"

"Accept," said the tiger. "And they will accept you. If you run you will fail. If you fight you will fall. You must only accept."

"I cannot go back!"

"You have to go back," said the tiger. "You are the eldest. You are not the only one; there's your brother and sister. And your mother and father had the same trouble and pain, but your mother was patient and your father was brave —the bravest in the school. It is for you to be patient like your mother and brave like your father, little one."

Joti looked at the ground and said nothing.

"It is hard," said the tiger. "But when they accept you they will accept you for always."

Joti stared at her feet and noticed for the first time how dark they were.

"The lessons are good," said the tiger. "Your teacher is good."

"Oh yes," said Joti. "I like the lessons. The teacher is nice. But she calls me Josie."

The tiger banged his paw on the ground so that Joti jumped. "That is a different matter," he said. "You'll have to stop that or it will last you all your life. Your mother's name is Premilla and they call her Milly. Your Aunt Halima was called Alma. And your Uncle Shamshir"—the tiger shuddered—"they called him Sam!"

Joti giggled and the tiger glanced at her sourly.

"You may think it funny now," he said. "And another thing, I would not wear that dress again. Wear your own name and your own clothes and they will understand you better."

Joti came down to breakfast the next morning in her white sulwa. "Look," she said. "I am me again."

Her mother looked relieved and Grandmother clucked approvingly as she plaited her hair. Her father said he would drive her to school.

During the drive Raj tried to think of something encouraging to say to his daughter. He knew what schools were like, but he did not know what to say to a seven-year-old who had dressed herself in a sulwa to be herself again.

"Tonight, Joti," he said at last, as he stopped the car, "I will bring home some lollies."

But already Joti was out of earshot. They were late and she could see that the class had gone in.

She hurried to her seat with hardly time to look at the girl who was sitting beside her on the side near the window. Miss Adams smiled at her and began to call the roll. "Dorothy Johnson."

"Present," said the girl beside Joti.

"Josie Kausheed."

Joti stood up, her legs shaking. "Please, miss," she said. "My name is Joti."

"I must have you down as someone else," said Miss Adams. "And Joti is too pretty a name to waste."

Joti breathed again and sat down. The tiger was always right.

At playtime Miss Adams showed them all a new game and helped them play it. Joti was shy about joining in, but soon she was laughing and leaping with the rest of them.

At lunch-time she sat with them defiantly and, ignoring their glances, began to eat her lunch.

"What are you wearing?" asked one of the girls.

"Sulwa," said Joti.

They thought about this.

"Why are you wearing it?" asked the red-headed girl. "Why don't you wear a dress?"

"Because the tiger said so," said Joti.

"What tiger?"

"My tiger," said Joti. "He lives in our garden."

"Oh, you are a fibber!" said the red-headed girl. "Tigers can't talk. And you couldn't have one living in a garden. He'd eat you up. And serves you right. You're a terrible fibber." The others did not need to think about this. They had found a word. "Fibber!" they called. "Fibber! Fibber!" Joti walked away, leaving the voices behind her. She sat at the end of the yard, and this time her tears were tears of anger. How dare they doubt her tiger!

"White pigs," she muttered. "White pigs."

"What's your tiger's name?" said a timid voice near her. It was Dorothy, the girl who sat beside her in school, who had been away the day before.

"He has no name", said Joti. "I call him Grandfather-Tiger-Sahib. He lives at the end of our garden. He is always lying on the bank near the river."

"I suppose," said Dorothy, sitting down beside her, "that's because he likes to swim. I would like a tiger. I've got no one to talk to, except Auntie."

"Where are your mother and father?"

"Mummy died," said Dorothy. "And Daddy works on a big ship and is always away."

"No mother!" said Joti horrified. "No mother at home!" And she offered the girl some of her lunch.

"Thank you," said Dorothy. "This tastes nice. Would you like one of my biscuits?"

"Thank you," said Joti. They sat side by side and ate. But Joti was remembering something. Was it something Tiger Sahib had said? No, it was Grandfather who said it. He had been talking about the trouble in India and Joti had listened.

"All men should be brothers," Grandfather had said, "and they become brothers by sharing. They share what they have —small things, big things— then they are brothers."

Joti grabbed Dorothy's arm. "We have shared our food," she shouted. "We are sisters, sisters!"

Joti ran home from school again, flew as though she had wings. She burst into the kitchen, forgot to take off her shoes and danced and shouted. "Grandmother! Mother!" she said. "You have to make more kababs tomorrow. I have to share them with my friend."

"Yes," said her mother. Yes, lots more." And she and Grandmother listened and smiled at one another while Joti chattered about her friend and her lessons and school.

She had so much to say that she forgot about her tiger. It was almost teatime when she remembered him. She ran down through the garden to talk to him. But he was not there. She called to him, but he did not come. She pushed aside the bushes with her hands, but she could not find him. And it was growing dark. Suddenly she knew that he would never come again. He had gone away because she did not need him; she was a schoolgirl now.

A LONG WAY

IT was an ordinary jumper; ordinary, but no one in the village had seen it. It was Nazit's secret. It was to go a long way.

Secretly, sitting in corners, she had worked at it—knitting it from Pakistani wool. It was for her younger son, the one in Australia.

Australia was a long way, but while she was shaping the wool Nazit felt that she and her boy were close. She knew that when he wore it he, too, would feel this, would feel that she and the village were close.

She had packed her basket. She had put into it three jars of chutney that everyone believed she was taking to her sister's house, but in her hands she held the soft wool jumper that was the real thing she was taking.

Her elder son's wife came to the door, and Nazit, turning quickly to hide, crushed the jumper into the basket, under the jars, out of sight.

"You will be back tomorrow?"

"Yes. Yes," said Nazit. "Tomorrow. My sister's house is not a long way." She half laughed at her cleverness.

She said good-bye then, and hurried from the house.

She hurried, looking backwards, looking from side to side, fearing to see her son, and not seeing anything else.

A holy singer and his two drummers were performing on the stone under the shisham-tree. A knot of workmen had gathered to watch.

Nazit avoided the crowd; Ali, her elder son, was too fond of singing.

It was not until she was out of the village, on the bank of the river under the wild cotton-trees and their spring-scarlet flowers that she stopped hurrying.

Nazit smiled, she was safe. The village and her son's fields were a long way off. She was on her own. She followed the wide road.

At the railway station at Mooltan, Nazit showed her savings to the ticket-seller.

"Will this," she said, "take me to Karachi?"

"No," said the ticket-seller, who was hot and tired. He went on scribbling on the paper in front of him. "B.A. (Lahore—failed)," he wrote.

He wrote it five times more. Then he screwed up the paper, threw it on the floor, and looked miserably out of his cage. The old woman was still standing in front of the grille. Now she was crying.

"How far?" she said. "How far to Karachi may I go? It is all I have."

For half a second the ticket-seller felt sorry for someone other than himself. "Mother," he began, but he remembered himself. "Why does an old woman like you need to look outside her village?"

"I have to," said Nazit. "I have to be in Karachi. How far, how far will this money take me?"

The ticket-seller felt tired again. It was impossible to converse with these peasants from the villages. He counted her money again, and pretended he was the teller in a European bank at Bombay.

He counted the money four times, but it was never more nor less; it was hardly worth counting.

"How far?" said Nazit.

"Don't interrupt," said the Bombay bank manager. "I am working." He counted the money again, and stacked it in bank-like piles—rupees (not many), annas (some), pice (a lot). "To Ranipur," he said.

Nazit was frightened. "Is it far? Is it far from Karachi?"

The ticket-seller knew only that it was the station before, but he couldn't say that, he was a University Man. He handed her a ticket.

"Not far," he said. He felt kind. "Not far at all."

Nazit sat on the platform. It was full of strangers.

She took the jumper from the basket, and she folded it carefully, fondling it, thinking all the time of Yaseem her younger son and of the Plan.

She remembered the day, miracles ago, when the Big Man had come to the village in the big black car. He had a drummer with him, and the drummer beat upon his drum until almost all of the village had gathered. Then the Big Man stood on the great stone, and told the people that he had brought them a notice. He nailed it to the shisham-tree. The notice told them of the Plan.

The Big Man explained that he was from the Big Government in Karachi and that there were other Big Governments in the world. He said that the Big Governments were friends, and they were friends who would help.

The villagers listened politely; some of the words were big, and some of them were new, and none of them meant anything at all. When the Big Man had finished they went back to their work.

But the words had meant something. Cars kept passing through the village, and Government men, in Western clothes, stopped to tell things. One of them said that Rufi, the barber's son, and Yaseem, Nazit's youngest, had worked so hard in the big school in Karachi that they could have scholarships and go a long way—to Australia.

No one understood. No one wanted to understand. "We have our ways," said the villagers. "They are our fathers' ways."

Rufi's father, the barber, forbade him to leave his country. "My son has his home," he said.

Nazit pleaded with her boy to stay. "You are the youngest," she said. "You are the one that is mine."

Then the Begum came to the village. She was an old lady with grey hair, but she stood very straight, and everyone knew that she was wise and good. She had helped them always. She explained to them about the Plan, and they listened.

"The old ways were good, but the new ways are better. They are a gift of goodwill. But we must work, all of us. We must help. We must let our children learn, so that they can teach others. We must let them go a long way, so that they can return. It is not a kindness. It is a goodness."

To her the villages listened. Her they believed. Rufi and Yaseem sailed from Karachi to Australia, and though Nazit cried for her boy, and the barber cried, too, they knew that it was good. Their Begum had said so.

And then Nazit had heard that the Begum was going to Australia, too.

Nazit made the jumper, the ordinary jumper, and she decided to take it to Karachi to the Begum, to ask her to give it to Yaseem so that it would be from his mother's hands and from the hands of the Begum who knew him.

She had to hurry. She had to tell lies, to say she would go to her sister's, to say that she would stay there the night. Ali, her elder son, would not have let her go to Karachi alone. He might have taken the jumper himself, and it would have been a thing not from her hands but from Ali's.

Ali would look for her when she did not return. The man at the station would tell him perhaps where she had gone. He would find her, in time, and he would bring her safely home, scolding and being ashamed that she had been alone on the road like a woman with no family. But that would not matter. Yaseem had gone his long way, and she would have gone her long way, too.

The train came in with smoke and great noise. It frightened Nazit a little, and the strangers frightened her, too. They jostled through the compartment doorways, pushing with their rolls of bedding and their bulky bundles.

Nazit sat in the crowded carriage, jammed between people.

The night came on, and though the nights were cool in all the world they were not cool there, and Nazit felt sick with heat—suddenly, old and tired. She sat though with open eyes. What if, in that carriage full of strangers, a hand had touched her basket, and the jumper had gone? What if her station came and she not heard its name?

Dawn came, and the minute after dawn was breathless and hot, but although the train had stopped many times it was not till then, that minute, that anybody called out, "Ranipur!"

It was a big station, and people were sleeping on it in its shade. Nazit would have slept, too, but she was afraid. She knew that thieves are found on railway stations.

Suddenly, cleverly, she had an idea. Half hiding in a doorway, she took the jumper from her basket and put it on under her sulwa-blouse.

She sat cross-legged on the station, her eyes ready to close just for a minute. A young girl was sitting near her. The girl was watching her husband. He was approaching the food-sellers, his eyes downcast, his manner timid. He was a Hindu. The sellers were Muslims. What if they would sell him nothing? What if they should give him little for his money? Two annas! It was all he had.

They sold him four chupatties and, gratefully, he thanked them. "Hindu boy!" They laughed at him. "Even Hindu boys must eat."

He walked confidently back to his wife, looking sure and tall, showing her the food and explaining how he had cleverly managed to get so much for his money. He began to laugh. She smiled, too, then she gestured towards Nazit; the hunched-up figure of an old woman almost sleeping.

A Muslim lady alone! He looked inquiringly at his wife. She put her eyes down modestly, then nodded. He went to Nazit, and touched her arm gently.

Starting, Nazit gazed up at him. But it was not a thief's face, only a Hindu boy. "Mother," he was calling her. "My wife and I . . ." He pointed proudly to the girl, and then continued, choosing his words carefully because he knew well that Punjabi Muslims are independent and ungracious, and that Hindus to them are often only Hindus. "I have foolishly bought too much food for us. My wife and I would be happy if you would take some with us."

Nazit looked at the girl with her lowered head and her gentle smile. She looked at the four chupatties. "I thank you, my son," she said. "You are good."

She sat with them and shared their little food. They talked like friends. They had been married a very little time. They had come the long way to Ranipur, because it was big and might want them. It might give them food and work. But the girl was frightened. It was all new.

Nazit told her to have faith. "It is all beginning," she said. "My son— my youngest son—he has gone a long way. He is with people he has never known." She told them about the Plan, the Begum's promises. "It will come true," she said. "Your children will learn and they will eat. They will do wonderful things."

All this time the girl had sat with her head down, even when she was speaking, but now she raised her head and smiled.

"Our children," said she. "Our children. We have been married two days!" She and her young husband, and Nazit, too—the three of them laughed like friends who knew.

The sun was higher now, and the Hindus rose to leave. Nazit took one of the jars of chutney from her basket. "A gift," she said. "My sons say my mango chutney is the finest in all the Punjab. It is possible they are right."

Nazit watched them go. Then she went to the station-master.

"How far?" she said. "How far to Karachi? Which way do I go?"

"This is the main road." He pointed. "If you followed it you'd come some time to Karachi. It's a long way."

Nazit hardly heard. Already she had turned to face the road. The sun climbed high and her walk grew faster. She was in a hurry to leave the town behind. After, afterwards, outside of the streets, then she would rest.

Women sat for coolness in the doorways that she passed. Some of them were churning curd to make butter. The sound of the churns echoed in Nazit's mind, reminding her of her own village and her own work undone.

She hurried—but her steps grew slower, no matter how hard she tried. On every little rise she stopped and looked ahead, hoping to see the city, but she saw nothing but broad road, huts by the way, another little village to pass through.

The sun was above her head now, and she had no shadow. She was tired, and the basket had grown heavy. She was hungry, too.

An old woman sat at the door of one of the village houses. She nursed a baby. "Sister," she called. "You have walked a long way. Come in and rest."

Inside the house was water for Nazit's dusty feet, a dish of pilau for her to eat, the baby to be looked at and the woman to be talked to.

She told her of Yaseem and of the jumper that was to go such a long way. She took it off and showed it. The woman cried out at the softness of the wool.

"Think of it!" said the woman. "Such a long way! My son, too—the father of my grandchild—he is in Canada. He is learning, too. Think of that! My husband was a sweeper. He and I were called chamars, we were untouchables. But our son now can be a doctor. Think of that! And his son— here with big eyes open—who knows what he can be?"

Nazit lifted the baby, and the two women wept. To them it seemed the world was flowering.

"Allah bless you," said Nazit as she moved to go. She put one of her jars of chutney on the table. "I have far to go".

"Ram, Ram. Peace be with you," said the woman. "It is not far. There is one more village, and then the city. The Christian village. It is called the Biscuit Tin."

It was late afternoon when Nazit came to the village and found the Biscuit Tin. It was a church on stilts. Its roof and walls were beaten tin. There was no one to be seen. She sat on the steps in the shade, and leant on the handle of her basket.

Inside in the tiny vestry the priest was dressing himself for Mass. He was trying not to remember his church in Madras, not to think of clean streets and cool buildings at all, not to envy whoever had it now with its regular few devoted parishioners.

He had no parishioners here, only people who lived in the parish—peasants, a few refugees. Most of them, Hindus, all of them polite, they thanked him for teaching their children. They came to Mass sometimes and listened. They were grateful and that was gratitude, but they had their own ways and his way was not theirs.

He had told the Bishop so, had written and told him: the conversion rate in this country is less than one in a million and probably none is a real conversion. But the Bishop from Ireland did not or would not understand. "It is possible," he replied, "that one in a hundred million is real, Father Wilton, and that possibility makes all effort good."

Father Wilton thought about it. He supposed it was true, but he doubted it, and he found it little comfort.

Tutting, he removed three oranges from the cupboard. It was typical of the visiting medical nuns to hide their little gifts in an inconvenient place. The oranges were on top of his chasuble.

They had not marked it, and he put it on. He went into the church thinking of the day's business—last rites for an old woman surrounded by family, crying and useless. They had repeated the prayers, but now they were out—they, and all the village, burning the wretched woman as though she were a pagan.

The church offended him. An old table for an altar—that was an insult to God, but he comforted himself with the thought that the Mass he was to say was the same as the Bishop's, the same as the Pope's. He intoned the words and told himself that he was in a cathedral. Afterwards, changed to mournful black, carrying the oranges, he made to leave the church, but the sun in the doorway glared into his eyes. Even the evening sun here was distastefully irreverent.

He moved to descend, and Nazit turned and looked up at him. He saw into her eyes. For a few seconds he stood humbly in her gaze. He dropped the oranges into her basket, and moved down the steps past her. Nazit watched him go, wondering what one said to a strange white man. She put the last of her jars of chutney on the step and, taking the oranges,, she walked over to the irrigation channel. She sat by it and bathed her feet as she ate the oranges. She thought of the old woman who had talked to her: this was the last village, this was not far from Karachi, this must be her last rest.

But it was far, a long way. The road went on and on, and Nazit followed it. At every turn, after every clump of trees, she hoped for the city, but it was not there. It was never there. Her eyelids kept closing as she walked. She wondered if Karachi ever was.

It was dark now, but the night was still and hot, and the sky seemed close and heavy on her back. She was sweating.

Her eyes were running, almost as though she were crying, but it was sleep.

She could not stop, could not stop. It was tomorrow the Begum was to go, was to go a long way, and Nazit must go her long way, too.

The clothes clung to her, and her almost-empty basket felt like a weight, but her feet moved more quickly.

The road wound round a hill, and suddenly, on the turn of the road, there were people everywhere—in tents and shelters, in poorest huts, people who cooked by open flame, children who ran naked between the fires, people who wore rags. They were refugees.

"Praise Allah!" said Nazit. "I am in good time. It is not near day and I am in Karachi." She went to a clump of guava-trees, and took the jumper from her basket. Again she put it on and hid it under her blouse. Everyone knew that refugees stole.

She sat there under the trees, and watched the children playing round the fires as her children had played, hand-in-hand, singing, their bodies gleaming. Thieves, she thought. Must they all be thieves?

It was morning when she woke, early morning. The first breath of the day moved on her face. She woke wondering for a moment where she was and why. "Laila," she murmured. That was her daughter-in-law's name. Why wasn't she near? Why wasn't she cooking? There were other people cooking. All round her were little fires, the smell of curry. "Laila, Ali," she said. Then she remembered.

"Eh, mother, mother," said a gnarled old man near her. "You don't belong here. You're not used to being on your own. Would you like some water?" He held an earthenware jug towards her.

Nazit took it from him and held it, looking at him. He was black as a Bengali, but he was smiling at her.

"You are kind," she said.

"I don't know about kind. I'm just a man who one day will be old."

Nazit smiled at him. "I am older than you, and I have come a long way," she said. "And I am wiser than you, because I know that everyone is kind."

The man laughed at her. "Where are you going, mother?"

"Where I am now—Karachi."

"This isn't Karachi. This is the cantonment, the refugee camp. We're miles from the city."

"But—" Nazit faltered. "The ship," she said. "I have to be there. When the ship sails—it sails this morning, before midday. Is there time?"

"Yes. There's time," he said. "You come with me. I am going in my cart, to the markets. I sell pots, jugs, anything that earth can make. You come with me, and I'd drive you there. The bullocks are faster than mountain rivers. Are you catching the ship?"

"No," said Nazit. "This is my place. But I am going to see the Begum."

The Begum stood by the ship's rail, and looked at the crowd that filled the wharf. Her son Selim stood by her and talked. Everything he said annoyed her. He was educated and Englishy and arty. Her two friends— Dr Haroon of Karachi Hospital, and Professor Shah, the philosopher from Lahore University—they talked, too, like old friends, with jokes and laughter. But the Begum hardly heard them, did not want to hear them. Everything they said was irrelevant. She was sure that in a moment either they or Selim would say (wittily), "*Bon voyage.*"

Bon voyage, she thought. *Bon voyage* to where, for what?

Her daughter had been in Australia for some time. She wrote home often, but recently the letters from Australia had been full of worries. The Plan might fail, its good work be undone. There were critics who said that it was silly, wasteful, uneconomic; that the country had causes of its own, that its people needed houses, and that its people's money was being thrown around overseas. What, they asked, have foreigners to do with us?

What, indeed? The Begum could see it all, understand it all. What had foreigners to do with her? The critics were right. Australians need have nothing to do with her people unless they wanted to be friends. And did they want to? How could a Begum know?

She clutched at her handbag irritably: it was full of notes for her Australian lecture tour — U.N.O. reports, health reports, hygiene reports, soil reports, irrigation reports—what do reports mean? Numbers. Statistics. Foreigners. Odd untidy things a long way off.

"*Ma mére*" said Selim. "*Ma mére*, the professor has spoken to you twice, asked you a question—twice! And you haven't answered."

"Your pardon," said the Begum. "Don't call me *ma mére*, Selim. Be English, if you can't be Pakistani. You were saying, Professor?"

Someone touched her arm and she turned.

"Nazit," she said. "Nazit! You came to see me off, to wish me well! But where is Ali, Laila?"

"I have come alone," said Nazit.

"Alone?" The Begum and her friends stared at her. Nazit was very old and a Muslim. "But, Nazit, how?" The Begum still held her, but now she held her away and looked into her red-rimmed eyes.

"I came in the train to Ranipur, and then I walked."

"You walked alone from Ranipur?" Selim was Pakistani enough to be shocked.

"Yes," said Nazit. "But last night I slept. A kind man drove me here today." She swayed. Almost she fell as she spoke, but the Begum held her.

"Sister," she said. "Child. I must call you child to come so far. You could have sent your wishes. Why, why did you come?"

Nazit handed her the jumper. "It is not a good jumper," she said. "But I made it for Yaseem, my youngest—Yaseem who is in Australia. Give it to him for me, from his mother's hands."

"I will give it to him," said the Begum. "I will find him and give it to him. I will tell him to love it. But you—you must now do as I say, exactly as I say."

"Yes," said Nazit. "Exactly as you say." She suddenly felt very old and very useless, wanting Ali and even Laila with all her irritating household ways.

"Selim," said the Begum, "you will send a telegram to Ali. You will tell him that Nazit is with you, in my house, safe. And then you will—"

"Mother! Mother!" said Selim. "I am an adult I have graduated. I know what to do. You are not supposed to lecture me."

"I can lecture others," said the Begum. "I will lecture to others."

The whistle was blowing. The voices all round were louder. Hands were beginning to wave.

"It is time for us to go," said the Professor.

"Bon voyage," said Dr Haroon.

"God," said the Begum, thinking her own thoughts, "God be with us all. God help us all."

"All," said Nazit "They all of them helped me with kindness. Everyone is kind—the Muslims, the Hindu, the Untouchable, the Christian, the Potter. They all of them helped me. They didn't know me, but they loved me. They helped me and I didn't know their names."

They all looked at her, but it was Selim who spoke—Selim who was educated and wrote poetry and was irritating.

"Mother," he said to Nazit, "what else should they do? They are your people, all your people. The world is your people."

The ship moved from the wharf, and the streamers broke. A cry went up from the crowd, and the Begum waved. My people, she thought. My people—Selim, the professor, the doctor, Nazit, the man and the woman, the babies in arms, my people. Our people.

On the wharf she saw the few wealthy and well-fed, the many thin and poorly dressed. So many were waving to her, so many were waiting for her... she stared at them, seeing a thin-legged child who was running through the crowd gathering streamers, to roll and sell again, a pregnant woman who was leaning on the custom-house wall. All, thought the Begum, all our people.

The ship moved from the bay.

In her mind the Begum saw the refugee camps, the hungry and the poor, the beaten and the lost. They are all our people, she thought, no matter who we are or what, no matter where they are or why, the world is all our people. She took the notes from her bag and tore them slowly, carefully, into four. She dropped the pieces onto the water. She watched them float, watched them swell, and sink. Reports, she thought. Statistics. Numbers. I will tell them— I will find the people, and I will tell them. I will go to the houses, the streets, the parks. I will find the people who are my people, and I will tell them how their people need. I will tell them how Nazit came to me a long way and how I, too, have come to them a long, long way.

The ship moved on, towards Australia, parting the sea, going quickly on its long, long way.